THE LAST GREEN LIGHT

A Novel

GEORGE MICHELSEN FOY

GUERNICA
World
EDITIONS

TORONTO–CHICAGO–BUFFALO–LANCASTER (U.K.)
2024

Guernica Editions Founder: Antonio D'Alfonso

Michael Mirolla, general editor
Scott Walker, editor
Cover design: Allen Jomoc, Jr.
Cover art: Emilie Gabriel, E-Design
Interior design: Jill Ronsley, suneditwrite.com

Guernica Editions Inc.
1241 Marble Rock Rd., Gananoque (ON), Canada K7G 2V4
2250 Military Road, Tonawanda, N.Y. 14150-6000 U.S.A.
www.guernicaeditions.com

Distributors:
Independent Publishers Group (IPG)
600 North Pulaski Road, Chicago IL 60624
University of Toronto Press Distribution (UTP)
5201 Dufferin Street, Toronto (ON), Canada M3H 5T8

First edition.
Printed in Canada.

Legal Deposit—First Quarter
Library of Congress Catalog Card Number: 2023951651
Library and Archives Canada Cataloguing in Publication
Title: The last green light : a novel / George Michelsen Foy.
Names: Foy, George Michelsen, 1952- author.
Series: Guernica world editions (Series) ; 77.
Description: Series statement: Guernica world editions ; 77
Identifiers: Canadiana (print) 20230583881 | Canadiana (ebook)
2023058392X | ISBN 9781771838870
(softcover) | ISBN 9781771838887 (EPUB)
Subjects: LCGFT: Novels.
Classification: LCC PS3556.O99 L37 2024 | DDC 813/.54—dc23

THE LAST GREEN LIGHT

A Novel

GUERNICA WORLD EDITIONS 77

Constantly bring to thy recollection those ...
who have been most conspicuous by the greatest
fame or misfortunes or enmities or fortunes of every kind;
then think, Where are they all now?
Smoke and ash, and a tale, or not even a tale.

—**Marcus Aurelius**, *Meditations, Book 1*

Chapter One

When I was on leave from the Navy during the last days of the Great War, I took a train across Italy to the South of France. I had learned enough French from previous journeys to understand most of the signs and advertisements there. "*La Quinquina Royal est un vrai trésor*" meant this quinine-laced apéritif was, in the opinion of advertisers at least, "a real treasure." "*Semez des pommes de terre pour les soldats, pour la France*" urged you to plant potatoes for the soldiers, and for France.

One of the signs I liked best, for its brevity and common sense, was posted near the tracks at level crossings and read, "*Un train peut en cacher un autre*"—"One train can hide another." It warned you to not pay heed solely to the express thundering toward you on the near track; not to cross as soon as it passed when another train, hidden by the first, might be roaring smoking speeding at you on the far track to crush you into oblivion.

I mention this in connection with the murder of the late Jim Gatz, better known as Jay Gatsby, and the love affairs notoriously connected with his death, all of which made headlines in the papers for a week or so last fall until other news of this turbulent time chased that tragedy into the gossip pages and finally to the shallows and back-eddies of our recall; so that for six months or more a mention of the name "Gatsby" might conjure, around New York at least, a foggy memory on the order of "Wasn't that the millionaire who was shot to death on Long Island—something to do with a woman, with shady deals?"—until at last Jay Gatsby passed from the public's memory altogether.

But not from mine.

—

My name is Jaan Laine, also known as Jon. I was probably the one person, outside his family in the Midwest, who by the time he died had known Gatsby the longest. I remember clearly when I first met him; and in a way, because this was the day (I learned later) he first adopted his new name, I met him at the moment of his birth, on a cloud-strewn morning in 1905 with a sharp wind blowing out of the northwest, on the yacht *Tuolomee* off Little Girls Point in Lake Superior. We were anchored there to allow the yacht's owner, Dan Cody, to rendezvous with one of his fancy women, who lived nearby in Saxon Harbor. I was on anchor watch in the wheelhouse when I spotted Gatz, or Gatsby, rowing hard in a fishing skiff from shore. As he came under the ship's gangway he shouted up at me that the weather was changing and the shallow ground off Little Girls Point was dangerous in a blow and we should move. The shouting drew Cody to the rail, and he asked the man to come aboard and explain himself.

Gatsby was very young then, maybe seventeen or eighteen. He was well-built and tan from working on the water; I remember a chestnut pompadour, a strong chin and a grin he spread like melted butter over everyone around. He carried himself with an offhand grace that seemed to belong to someone different, a man of high standing who had ended up fishing the southwest lake by accident, or maybe on a lark.

And he was a great talker. I am of Finnish stock and not gifted in that department, so I watched in some admiration as Gatsby forged a tale of storm, shipwreck and his own expertise that seemed to imply, in form rather than content, that even the worst obstacles must waste to clinker in a furnace of optimism, the location of which he alone knew the secret. He used his hands while talking, not ostentatiously like an Italian but subtly, changing their angle to the wrists and back, as if marking time with his words. By the time he'd finished even Cody, who had made his fortune as a prospector in the Nevada silver fields and was tough-minded about everything except women, had fallen for his charm and enthusiasm, and asked me to sign him on as deckhand. It so happened we'd been a man short since Cleveland.

I don't mean to imply that Gatsby was a fraud or charlatan, as many have suggested, although it's true that when Jay died he and I were engaged in a game that was far from above-board. He knew his way around a foredeck and worked hard on *Tuolomee*, so that after sixteen months he was promoted to second mate under myself and Captain Eriksen. Gatsby and I were friends, at first—not close, but friends in the way you become when both are young, agreeable and rely on each other day in, day out to keep a ship running and safe. We steamed through the Saint Lawrence that year, then down to the West Indies, and crossed the Atlantic to French North Africa. The next year we crossed back to Florida, and to Panama.

But Gatsby had a plan which did not include working on yachts forever, and he started implementing that plan from his very first day on *Tuolomee*. He did so by conversing with Dan Cody every chance he got, and doing odd jobs for him, such as locating women in different ports, that had nothing to do with the ship; and so became, after a couple of years, the old man's confidant and private secretary. By the time Cody's former lover, Ella Kaye, came back on the scene and *Tuolomee* was laid up, Gatsby had acquired, as if by osmosis, the old man's jargon of bank finance and the commodities trade; riding a train of speech that, while it still rolled on the great plain vowels of his Midwestern home, pulled a cargo of somewhere else: as if, instead of his few weeks at Saint Olaf College, he'd been educated in a school stuffed with lacquered oak and silver tea services equidistant from Newport, Chicago, and the Isle of Wight.

It was not a change that did our friendship any good, and here perhaps I should point to why, by saying something about myself. I was born in Duluth to immigrants from Finland, which was then a colony of Russia. My father had been a ferryman and his brother, my Uncle Tai, worked in a ship chandlery in the Ullanlinna area of Helsinki. After running into trouble for anti-government activities, which in those days could mean something as tame as saying the Tsar was a bit out of touch with his subjects, they emigrated to Minnesota—like half of Scandinavia, it seemed, they had cousins there—and when they got to Duluth my uncle naturally sought work in one of the supply businesses that were springing up, like chanterelles in rain, to service the Twin Ports. After Tai found a job he hired my father to run a boat that ferried goods to vessels anchored off Minnesota Point. Around the time I came along they had started their own chandlery, Laine Brothers, in a brick warehouse on West Superior Street; and it grew fast with the ports, with the increasing number of ships come to haul Dakota wheat and Mesabi iron ore; ships that needed great quantities of paint, oil, rope, turnbuckles, charts, canvas and all the other myriad goods Laine Brothers kept in stock. The chandlery grew so fast that the brothers started to disagree over how to manage a company that now employed over fifty workers. Tai wished to expand into coal and lumber whereas my father, more cautious, thought they should stick to the business they knew—till eventually, with little acrimony and less talk, my uncle bought his brother out.

I was eighteen at that point, and going to the same college Gatsby would attend five years later. But whereas Gatsby only spent a couple of weeks at Saint Olaf, I studied there for over a year, happily absorbing philosophy, history and other disciplines that would never get me a job in the real world—until one day in November of sophomore year my father, who had invested all his profits from the chandlery (on Tai's advice) in a new railway company: the Mesabi, Duluth and Chicago; arrived unannounced to tell me the railway had gone bust and taken the family's savings, and my tuition money, with it.

Though I was hardly aware of it at the time, this was the tail end of the 1901 financial panic, one of the many crises of capitalism that skewed the course of my life, among others', in the infant years of the new century. My uncle found me work on one of his supply boats, but it was clear that the good jobs at Laine Brothers must go to his sons. Counseled by a childhood friend who worked on a tug-boat that Laine Brothers supplied, I soon took a more lucrative job on his tug—a job whose side-effects, curiously, would later rekindle, then cool, my friendship with Gatsby.

—

For the Duluth tugs in 1903 were a hotbed of revolution. The steel and railway trusts had succeeded in banning unions like the Knights of Labor and AFL from most mining, shipping and railroad operations; but half the tugboatmen of Duluth, many of whom were Finns like Seppo and me, rejected an open shop. A tugboatmen's strike the year before had triggered a running feud between scab boats and union tugs that resulted in near-collisions, rammings, even the occasional gunfight, as we raced to be first to dock a ship. The McCrae Co. tugs were union; Seppo and the crew of the *Alice McCrae* were members of both the Duluth-Superior Watermen's Guild and of the Finnish Socialist Federation; and when the Federation joined the International Workers of the World we joined the IWW as well, and marched with heads high through Duluth in solidarity with workers everywhere.

By then my parents had sold their house and moved to a cottage in Superior. By then I too had moved, to lodgings on St. Croix Avenue, a stretch of Scandinavian saloons, boarding houses, saunas and brothels between the high ground and the Duluth ship canal. The contrast between mansions rising in my old neighborhood to house officers for Carnegie's steelworks, Morgan's banks and Rockefeller's railways, and the scrawny kids and struggling charwomen living in cold, rat-sick rooms in Finn Town—together with the political fervor of Seppo and the rest of our crew—soon brought me, singing with the passion of the newly converted, into the choir of a revolutionary movement we were certain must soon succeed.

But the revolution never came. A year later Seppo and another McCrae engineer were ambushed by a scab crew outside a saloon on Rice's Point. Seppo was stabbed in the stomach and died, in great pain, in the dirt of Garfield Avenue. Jack McCrae sold his fleet to a company controlled by US Steel; his crews, blacklisted by the other tug companies, got jobs ashore or left town. Disillusioned and broke, I went back to Laine Brothers for a job, one week before Captain Eriksen, newly arrived in port, placed an order for supplies and mentioned to Uncle Tai that the steam yacht *Tuolomee* was in need of a deckhand.

Chapter Two

Ten years and a world war after leaving *Tuolomee* I heard from Gatsby again. I was working for Laine Brothers once more, in Finn Town as usual; lying in bed, still as a stunned pike, on a Thursday noon as I nursed a hangover from the bathtub gin they sold in the back room of Virtanen's grocery store; wondering hazily and for the hundredth time, to the extent I could wonder through the scrim of headache and nausea, why I hadn't yet used my deck-knife to slit my veins and end it all. I was putting off the moment when I must get up and drag myself to the chandlery for the late shift when I heard the wheeze and shuffle and the creak of warped pine boards that meant Mrs. Ojala was heaving her bulk upstairs, probably to yell at me about the rent, which was late since I had spent part of it, again, at Virtanen's. Instead of yelling at me over money, though, she shrieked: "Message for you, Laine, dey come from your uncle"; and I knew I had finally gotten the sack.

But I was wrong. It was a telegram, and it was from Gatsby.

TO JON LAINE, C/O LAINE BROS CHANDLERY, DULUTH, it read. NEED YOU HERE FOR GREAT JOB STOP GUARANTEE $350 A WEEK STOP SEE MR WOLFSHIEM MANDALA HOLDING DAVIS ALUMINUM BUILDING NEW YORK NY BEFORE JUNE 8 STOP URGENT REPLY IMMEDIATELY

STOP TRAVEL FUNDS FOLLOW STOP LOOKING
FORWARD SEE YOU OLD SPORT STOP JAY GATSBY

I stared at the buff Western Union paper, head pounding, not believing. Cody's large and luxurious yacht; Gatsby with all his youthful hope and exuberance, seemed so unreal, so impossibly far away from me now. I felt as if I had escaped into sunlight for a few years on *Tuolomee*—on my subchaser, too, for fifteen months in the Navy during the war—only to sink back into a lifetime of melancholy, poverty and bleak Minnesota weather from which flight, I had finally accepted, was beyond my power.

And $350 a week was impossible, too. I was making $42 a week at Laine Brothers. No one I knew, except for Uncle Tai, made more than sixty.

It was the "old sport" that kept me from tearing up the telegram as a bad joke. "Old sport" was an expression Cody had used and that Gatsby picked up from the old man along with his mid-Atlantic accent: I think Jay had tried it out on me to work his tongue around it himself.

Paradoxically, a second factor that helped convince me was the vast improbability of a $350 wage for someone as unskilled as Jon Laine. Although unlike Gatsby I'd learned nothing about the financial world on *Tuolomee*, I wasn't a total fool and I knew a wage this high must mean something illegal: something to do, most likely, with the black-market trade in liquor that had exploded ever since the Volstead Act made selling it a crime.

I stared at that telegram for a good twenty minutes, believing and dismissing it in turn; listening to Mrs. Ojala downstairs scream at some kid she suspected of stealing a potato. It might have been the potato that finally got me out of bed. I dressed and walked to the outhouse and was sick. At the nearby pump I doused my head repeatedly in cold water.

Finally I walked downtown to the Western Union office and sent back a reply: the single word, YES.

After that, I dragged myself to the station and looked up the schedule of trains for New York City.

I arrived in New York on a late spring morning of wind and rushing clouds: warmer, but otherwise not unlike the weather on the day I first met Gatsby. Shifting cirrus and shafts of sunlight turned the glass domes and white columns of Pennsylvania Station into a moving picture of heaven on a day the angels waltzed. I had never seen anything as vast and febrile as that station and the crowds surging through it and along the avenue to which I was directed by the Pennsylvania Railroad's information booth.

The Davis Aluminum building was near Times Square. It was one of the shorter skyscrapers around but its door was protected by alabaster pilasters carved like twirled candy. Filigree of polished brass decorated the Moorish arches inside. A guard stopped me as soon as I came through the doors and, when I asked for the Mandala Holding Company office, looked me up and down as if to figure out what con this bum was working. I suppose he had reason. I'd been traveling for four days with little sleep and nowhere to shave properly; my hat was shapeless and sweat-stained; my one suit, which was not of the best quality to begin with, had frayed at cuffs and collar, and my bag was the same threadbare duffel bag I had on *Tuolomee*. But in the end he admitted, grudgingly, that the office I sought was on the eighth floor, and when I got there the elevator boy pointed to a door marked "Mandala Holding / By Appointment Only" and I walked in.

Another aspect of New York that had struck me the moment I got off the train was the women. I had never, even on the French Riviera, seen so many pretty girls in one place before. Duluth has its share of Scandinavian blondes, dark-skinned beauties, and red-haired women from Ireland, but they are scattered thinly across the landscape like everything else in the Midwest. In New York they flocked and fluttered thick as pigeons, or so it seemed, and wore skirts six inches higher above the ankles than in Minnesota.

The woman who looked up at me when I walked into Wolfshiem's office was as pretty as the rest. She had a small face with strong cheekbones, sarcastic lips, and very large, night-col-ored eyes, and black hair that burst in curls from under a sea-hued bonnet. Her calves shone like marble sculptures through the well of her desk. A cigarette smoldered boldly in her ashtray; the office, which held as well as her desk two potted trees, a cuspidor, a couch of cracked leather and a pair of armchairs, was misted with smoke. A man's voice, indistinct, percolated from a door of frosted glass be-hind her. Those eyes braised me up and down with more suspicion than the guard's. She frowned and said, "An' who the hell are you?"

"I'm here to see Mister Wolfshiem," I replied.

"He's not here."

I gestured at the door, which read "Director." The man behind was still talking. The woman shrugged.

"You got an appointment?"

"Nuh," I said. "No."

She picked up her cigarette, dragged at it, and looked back at what she was typing.

"Come back when you got one."

I laid Gatsby's telegram next to the ashtray. She glanced at it, muttered "Oh," picked up the telegram, went through the frosted glass; and came out a minute later followed by a sleek, compact man with receding black hair and a way of looking at you from the side.

"You're Laine," the man said. "I'm Meyer Wolfshiem." Without turning to the woman he said, "Stella, get Mister Laine some coffee, will you? Then call Gatsby and tell him his friend is here."

—

I did not see Gatsby that day—he was not in town, Wolfshiem said, eyeing me crabwise with an expression of incredulous distaste. "If you're going to work for Gatsby, you will have to dress better than that."

Wolfshiem himself was dressed like a bank president, in a well-cut wool suit, a silk bow tie, a gold watch-chain and shoes that reflected light like the slippers of a fairy-tale princess. His hair was pomaded and neatly cut, except for the nostrils, which sported tufts that clashed with the sleekness of his overall appearance; perhaps he kept his nose-whiskers long, mustaches having gone out with the Kaiser, to distract from a mole situated in the exact middle of that vertical gutter between lips and nose. His nose was curiously flat, as if he'd been punched, hard, just below the forehead. He smoked continuously and smiled almost as often. He told the secretary to guide me to my hotel. As soon as possible, he added, she should take me to Wanamaker's and buy me a couple of decent suits.

When he leaned to stub out a cigarette in Stella's ashtray his jacket opened, revealing a blue-black pistol holstered on his belt. He straightened, closed the jacket, nodded without quite looking at me, and went back into his office.

Stella led me four streets from the Davis Aluminum Building to the Metropole, a hotel whose foyer contained several fathoms of varnished panels, cut-glass light fixtures, vaulted ceilings, and tables of well-dressed men and women drinking coffee as they laughed and argued. The gay rhythms of a Dixieland band pulsed down a set of stairs a dozen feet wide.

Stella had not exactly warmed to me during our walk. That glimpse of the gun at Wolfshiem's belt had towed back worries about what kind of job Gatsby wanted me to do, but when I asked her about it on the way she refused to answer; keeping her distance, looking at me sideways as Wolfshiem had, as if to resolve the contradiction between whatever credit her boss might invest in Jon Laine, and the low-brow reality of the man. But as we waited for the concierge to find a room she started making small talk, and even smiled at me in a way that, albeit distant, set my chest to throbbing. It had been a long time since a woman smiled at me like that.

Then a bellhop led me to the elevators, to a room on the sixth floor with a neatly made-up bed and a sink from whose taps water both hot and cold flowed when you twisted them; and a fan that mixed the warm air inside with warm air from a window and peered over roof-tar and water tanks and a thousand chimneys belching smoke and steam, and various inexplicable metal structures, and a glimpse of the elevated railway, and another angle of clouds, and electrical signs in yellow red blue that flashed "Reach for a Lucky Instead of a Sweet," "Wear HoleProof Hosiery," and "Buy Turkish Trophies (Why pay more?)."

Even from this high up the sound of automobile horns, train wheels and the overwhelming hubbub of humanity saturated the air so densely, you had to wonder how the wind could blow at all.

I dropped myself on the bed, reflecting vaguely that on my first evening in New York I ought to hit the town. I longed to hear the band downstairs close-up, for I'd heard New York was as good as Chicago for jazz music. I wanted a cigarette, since I had run out of smokes before Albany. I desired, quite fiercely, a glass of gin, which I could now afford since Stella, on Mister Wolfshiem's orders, had advanced me five dollars for walking-around money.

I ached to watch women stride in their tight, calf-length dresses in that way they had here, as if the petty rules of the world outside New York had no traction upon them. I would rest for ten or fifteen minutes then go out, I told myself, closing my eyes. When I opened them again it was the next morning and someone was banging loudly on the door.

Chapter Three

Gatsby blew into my hotel room loud and abrupt as a white squall. "You made it, old sport!" he cried, taking both my hands in his, then strode to the window and opened it as wide as it would go. The room, I realized with embarrassment, was stuffy despite the still-churning fan, and stank of sweat. I was conscious of my swampy breath; of my shirt and pants, already stained from years of use, now damp and wrinkled from being slept in.

I was groggy from sleep and from dreams in which Wolfshiem's secretary, in the form of a red electric sign forty feet high, pointed her boss's gun at me and whispered words I could not make out. But the sharp delight of seeing Gatsby after so many years pierced through all that. Though his hair was shorter, and the clothes he wore were very different from the sailor uniforms on *Tuolomee*, the generous chin and sharp blue eyes, the simmered smile and fencer's stance were exactly the same. And he was as tan as he'd been on the ship.

"We're going to have real fun with this, Jon," he said in a more serious tone. "Wait till I tell you the whole deal."

He started explaining "the whole deal" fifteen minutes later as we drove through the streets of Manhattan in a car that was bigger and more luxurious than any I'd ever seen let alone ridden in. It was a cream-yellow Rolls-Royce, a phaeton that looked like a miniature Versailles of silver grille and chrome headlamps: it had wheel-guards curved like the Arc de Triomphe, running boards long as regret, belted luggage lockers and hat boxes, and a silver-winged angel at the car's snout to breast the cosmos.

The top was down and I sat beside Gatsby while he drove, holding my hat against the winds of our passage as we wove around horse-drawn carriages, trolleys, and trucks; at once exhilarated and terrified by the speeds Gatsby attained whenever the avenue cleared.

Behind us, on a green leather seat next to a bag of golf clubs, slouched a young woman who had been waiting in the car and whom Gatsby had introduced as Jordan. I'd got only a quick impression of her: a cloche hat, silver as the phaeton's grille and scaled like fish-skin; a pair of eyes that were gray and slightly slanted; a fringe of hair the color gold would be if gold drank milk. She wore a dress, tight and white, that barely broke a sweat to cover smallish breasts. A scarf of white silk, decorated with a line of blue dolphins (all smiling drunkenly), concealed half her face.

"I suppose you've realized, this is bound to be a bit of an adventure?" Gatsby yelled, accelerating around a streetcar.

"I still don't know what you want me to do," I shouted back.

"Meyer didn't say anything? Typical!"

We stopped at an intersection where a pair of horse-drawn wagons, one carrying crates and the other barrels marked Brooklyn Ash Hauling, had got snarled up and blocked the avenue. Men were shouting, gesticulating the way men do when they argue with other men about how to solve an utterly irrelevant technical problem. The horses, too, had no intention of backing down. The woman in the rear seat remarked with great feeling, "Lordy, how I hate horses!" A ragged boy ran up and asked for money, another tried to sell us a newspaper. Gatsby turned toward me.

"I'll give it to you straight, old sport," he said quietly. "Meyer has bought two steamers to bring liquor from Canada to the three-mile limit. I have a new speedboat, and I want you to skipper her, and run the hootch into Long Island. The government says this is illegal." He looked at me carefully as the fingers of his left hand drummed softly on the wheel. "But you're not too fond of the government, as I recall."

"No," I said, after a pause, and this was true. I could have added that I wasn't too fond of rich bootleggers selling gin at extortionate prices to the proletariat, but the anger I used to feel about this sort of injustice had been broken by what happened to Seppo in Duluth. It was a disillusionment that had led me to join the Navy when the old Jon Laine, a card-carrying member of both the Finnish Socialist Federation and the IWW, would have opposed a war fought by workers against other workers for the greater profit of capitalists. The war had brought about a loss worse than Seppo's, and finished the process of turning me into a political cynic— someone with no hard beliefs outside of self-preservation; the kind of man, I supposed, who swelled the ranks of mercenary bands and criminal organizations the world over.

Gatsby was still staring at me. "The way we set it up, old sport, there's almost no risk, and the money's amazing—just amazing. That three hundred 'n fifty a week's just a start, you'll get a bonus each time—"

I glanced at the woman in back. She was frowning at the wagon drivers, who had now come close to trading blows, but I had a feeling she was listening. "It's okay," Gatsby said, "she's in on the game." And now he smiled that smile of his. And the feeling I'd had the first time I met him, of an optimism strong and irresistible as a speeding train, touched me even more powerfully than it had on *Tuolomee*'s deck.

I suppose, given how low I'd fallen on St. Croix Avenue—given the sense of dislocation, and amazement, that traveling for four days halfway across the continent to this city of towers, lights, and headlong women imparted—I was more vulnerable to the charm Gatsby purveyed than I'd ever been in my life. Hope seemed to chip off him in tiny glittering shards to sparkle in the air around us.

I sensed a new edge to his hope, too, something even sharper and keener than before, but in the moment it only felt like an addition to the smile's power, an extra slice to his cut.

And I *wanted* that. I craved a piece of that power. I yearned to catch some of those bright shards. I longed to cup my hands and drink his hope like gin so I could craft a new life for myself, here, now. And I knew I would accept his offer, just as I'd known it in the back of my soul when I replied "yes" to his telegram.

"Maybe he's against it morally," Jordan said quietly. "Maybe you should have told him first."

"No," I said, looking at her. The scarf had slipped. Despite everything going on in my head I still noticed the way her mouth was wide and mobile enough to pitch a question at one end and field its answer at the other.

"You can count me in," I said.

—

Five minutes later the waggoners reached a compromise and the avenue cleared. We sped north, then east across a bridge whose steel towers and cables seemed high enough to throw a line over the sun and all its bleached-blue heavens and lift Manhattan anywhere.

And only a half hour later we entered Hell; or rather, what would remain of Hell if the devil, being otherwise engaged, let its eternal fires die.

Hell did not come without warning. The streets we drove through had become progressively rougher, the houses of soot-stained brick increasingly shabby, the kids more ragged. The air went smoky, and behind us the city's towers faded. But when we broke clear of houses and dived under the abutments of a railroad bridge spanning a foul and stinking creek, the landscape that met my eyes then seemed to fill my soul, albeit recently opened to the possibility of a new life, with an awe so strong and dreadful I felt as if I had truly entered a netherworld from which ambition and other sunny possibilities stood small chance of making it out alive.

This was a country of spent fire and burnt-out hope: great hills and valleys of dust, slag and clinker, flood-plains and moraines of smoking coke and fine ashes; the kind of ash, I now realized, that one of those crashed wagons in Manhattan must have been haul-ing. As we entered this country the ash, of black and dun and every variation in color between, soared in bluffs fifty feet above us on both sides; and we followed a line of cars, trucks, wagons, push-carts, all hauling the remains of what had once burned to keep the city moving, down an ashen track that led us deep into this blistered land. Smoke and dust rose around us in a hot fog, and soon the three of us were coughing; even through the fog I glimpsed half-naked figures walking, stooping, digging, scrambling, sere as the ash they shoveled, charred as the corpses of fire victims, dark as the damned in every illustration of the underworld I'd ever come across.

When I glanced behind me I saw Jordan was lying on her back across the rear seat, the dolphin scarf now wrapped entirely around her face.

And Gatsby, beside me, was laughing, waving away the dust and smoke with his boater and coughing at the same time. "It's *perfect!*" he shouted between coughs, turning to grin at me. "It's perfect, just wait and see."

After a few minutes, which felt more like hours, and cued by some unseen landmark, he steered the car out of the line of ash carriers and we emerged into relatively clearer air, on a track that ran between the land of ashes and the broadened creek to a couple of large, decrepit-looking structures and a rotten wharf, all built of black wood, leaning beside the water.

Three barges were moored at a final curve in the creek, beyond which the chromed waters of a small bay danced to a westerly wind, impossibly bright when seen from this vantage point; impossibly distant too. The smell of mud and old fish, seaweed and drains now mingled with that of dead fires. A battered Buick with a large "For Sale" sticker in the window was parked beside the farthest structure, which bore a cracked, half-effaced sign reading "… gio & Sons … & Lumber."

Rats fled our wheels as Gatsby parked his rolling palace, now covered with a thin film of soot, beside the flivver. He knocked twice, then once, then twice more on a wooden door; which shortly afterwards was opened by a tall black man in an oil-stained shirt and what looked like Navy uniform pants—who nodded, lowered the shotgun he was carrying, and stood aside to let us in.

The building we entered had no windows. Its interior was lit only by daylight coming from a high, thin opening at the far end and through numerous chinks between the walls' planks, as well as by two electric bulbs hanging from a rafter. This weak light gleamed on an expanse of water, smooth and dark as motor oil and framed by pilings; gleamed also on the varnished trim of a large, elegant motor yacht moored between walkways tacked to each side of the building.

"There she is," Gatsby said, and walked down the dock to the boat's stern. "The *Daisy.*" When I followed he slapped me on the shoulder, and his mouth stretched again in that engaging grin. "Here's your new command," he said, and I felt it again, that extra charge of hope I'd sensed in him earlier, thrumming like a small, precise motor geared to the greater engine of his nature. It brought a light voltage to his voice that I would have liked to think was driven by delight in seeing his former shipmate again, by offering him a job; but even then I sensed it came from somewhere else.

—

"You haven't seen anything till you've seen this baby open up." The man in Navy pants, whose name was Marcus Fayerweather, shook his head in admiration. "We're waiting for a new jet for one of the carburetors, it should get here tomorrow or the next day, Wilson says—then you'll see." He gazed at me intently, as if I might be inclined to doubt him; but I doubted nothing.

It was the evening of the day Gatsby and Jordan Baker had picked me up at the Metropole and showed me the *Daisy*. So much had happened over the last eight hours, so much I could never have imagined possible even yesterday morning, let alone a week ago when I received Gatsby's telegram, that if Fayerweather had told me America was a great cloudberry tart and the Atlantic was French Cognac I would have at least kept my mind open to the possibility.

We were sitting at a booth in a twenty-four-hour coffeeshop that proclaimed itself, with more cheek than conviction, a diner. It stood uncomfortably near the foul creek separating us, just barely, from the land of ashes. The coffeeshop was one of three attached, two-story buildings of yellow cement lining an otherwise sparse score of dirt-road and telephone poles between the creek—known, both appropriately and not, as the Flushing River—and the first houses of Flushing, Queens. One building sheltered the coffeeshop, another an automobile repair garage and filling station, the third a warehouse. A couple of used cars, and the half-dismantled skeleton of a Pierce-Arrow, lay behind the garage. All the buildings belonged to the operation Wolfshiem and Gatsby were running; everyone here worked for them. I had got the rundown from Gatsby as he showed me around the yacht.

There were three key elements to Gatsby's scheme. The first was a pair of small, steam-powered coastal freighters—old, Clyde-built and registered with the British Board of Trade—that would each load several thousand cases of Scotch whisky and English gin in the French islands of Saint Pierre and Miquelon, off Newfoundland, where the trade in booze was legal. The freighters, which Gatsby had told me belonged to Wolfshiem, would bring the liquor to Long Island Sound, to an area twenty miles long and more than three miles away from the shores of both Connecticut and New York State. Being over three miles from land made the area international waters, where a ship registered in Britain or in any other country besides the United States could not be boarded or apprehended by US authorities without causing an international incident.

"It's on the books, old sport," Gatsby had told me. "Wallace versus Providence and Stonington Steamship Company, Boston Circuit, 1882: the middle of Long Island Sound is the High Seas. Not a case I'd care to argue in court, mind you—but we won't have to."

He wouldn't have to because of the second element in Gatsby's scheme, which was a bosun's mate in the US Coast Guard head-quarters in Manhattan who was earning three-hundred dollars a week in cash from Wolfshiem. In exchange for such riches he wrote down the secret weekly schedule for the two Coast Guard cutters patrolling Long Island Sound; this copy he left at an agreed time between specific pages in a certain hymnal in a downtown Manhattan church for one of Wolfshiem's people to pick up.

And the third element was the *Daisy*, a two-year-old motor yacht refitted and repowered to Gatsby's specifications by the Scopinich boatyard in Freeport, Long Island. It was fifty-two feet long and fairly narrow in the beam, built for luxury as well as speed. Even in the gloom of the boathouse sheltering it I could see *Daisy* was a pretty thing, with a sharp bow carved in at water level to slice through waves, and scooped in its after portion to let the wake flow out more freely.

It had a saloon, with cherrywood table and settees under a generous wheelhouse forward, and a second cabin aft. The decks were Filipino teak; the gunwales, cabin paneling and outside trim were all mahogany, shellacked to a crystal shine. These, along with bronze fittings, portholes, and instruments, had reflected the oil lamp Fayerweather held as we followed Gatsby through the boat.

"But all this is for show," Gatsby said cheerfully, patting a gleaming counter in the after cabin. "To pretend she's just my yacht." He opened a hatch in the cabin's bulkhead and tripped nimbly down a tight companionway. "It's still a yacht, Jay," the woman objected while following him just as nimbly. "You can't hold it against a girl if she has to work for a living." Jordan's vowels, I noticed for the first time, were stretched, as if each word had molasses in it. This, I knew, was how people talked down South. When I descended the steps I found myself in a space that took up most of the boat's rear section and was filled to cracking by three large engines painted in red, silver and glint; by a man as well, who seemed to be embracing, under a pair of oil lamps, the top of the starboard machine.

"Wilson!" Gatsby had called, waving at the man, who climbed off his engine as we came in. He was tall and wide and to the extent I could make out in the feeble light, good-looking; he had a sheaf of light brown hair, a doll-like nose, pale and freckled skin, and small, gin-colored eyes that flicked between our faces almost nervously. His forehead bore a swipe of oil; he rubbed his hands, which were even more grease-smeared than his face, on a filthy rag; and in the half-dark, stooping against the low ceiling, he seemed almost inhuman, like a creature built for work underground, although this impression might well have come to me because of the proximity of Hell.

"Go on, Wilson," the woman said, "give him the lyrics, not just the tune."

"Ya mean the engines?" Wilson asked, glancing uncertainly at Jordan; and when she nodded, he picked up a couple of wrenches lying on the deck and, looking at them for inspiration, said, "Well, Liberty engines, they're—they were aircraft engines. Uh, twelve-cylinder, four-hundred horse, they used 'em in the war, in the De Havilland aeroplane—"

"Tell him how fast, George," Gatsby interrupted. Slapping me on the shoulder he said, "This is her new captain, I told you." And Wilson almost bowed to me, or to Gatsby, not fearfully but in a way that seemed to indicate he had no doubts about who were bosses in his world and who workers, and what the role of workers was inevitably to be. This from the start made me a little contemptuous of him. It was a feeling I would later regret.

The *Daisy*, Wilson continued—and now a worm of pride crawled up his voice—could move at just over forty knots or forty-six mph flat-out, unloaded; even fully laden it cruised at twenty-five knots, faster than anything the Coast Guard had to chase it with, assuming the Coast Guard was around to give chase at all.

Fayerweather opened a door in a forward bulkhead and I saw that everything under the cabins' deck and all the way forward, with the exception of copper fuel tanks and pipes on each side, and a chain locker in the bow, was empty space. Cargo could be stacked on a narrow deck between the boat's wooden ribs. The *Daisy*'s innards harbored the same smell *Tuolomee* had, of wood and varnish, salt and oil, mixed here with an aftertaste of gasoline. This hold would contain, Gatsby said, over two-thousand cases of top-notch British booze.

Then, winking at me, he asked us to move away from the door. He closed it, then opened a locker that had been concealed behind the door's panel. Through the shadows I made out a glower of barrel, magazine, and stock: a Colt-Browning machine-gun was pegged to the locker's back, over a box of ammunition labeled "US ARMY."

"Just in case, old sport," Gatsby said cheerfully.

The tour had brought us back to the wheelhouse—all except for Wilson, who'd returned to his engine. We stood by the compass and controls, looking through the windows facing forward. The boat's sharp bow, the only part blessed by daylight streaming through a gap above closed gates leading to the creek, seemed desperate to me: longing to leave this place, to surge into the wind-wild ranges of its true environment.

I felt, all at once, a corresponding need to touch the wheel and the engine throttles, as I used to aboard the *Alice MacRae*, and on *Tuolomee* also; but I held back. It seemed a gesture both too intimate and too possessive for a new captain to make.

Gatsby had left, with Jordan Baker, five minutes later. "Fayerweather and Wilson will drive you to the garage," he said: slapping his thigh now, his usual energy multiplied by a sudden, almost desperate impatience. "You're staying there, you see—at the warehouse, and they will fill you in on things like fuel and charts, and Meyer will give you details of the run.

"I cannot," he added, smiling at me with his usual warmth, tempered only by this new impatience, "I *cannot* be seen around the garage at all, especially with my automobile." He jerked a thumb toward the boathouse entrance. "Basic precautions, old sport.

"And speaking of precautions"—he lowered his voice a notch—"I'd rather you didn't mention *Tuolomee* to anyone. Far as they're concerned, anyone but Jordan here, you didn't know me before, right? You just answered an advertisement." He was still smiling but those blue eyes fixed me with an intensity that seemed to demand an answer, and though uncertain of why our past needed to be kept secret, I nodded. He handed me an envelope then and walked off, followed by the woman.

I followed them outside. The sunlight, even filtered by floating ash and dust, blinded me to the point where it took a few seconds to see Jordan and Gatsby had already boarded the phaeton, the engine of which coughed to life. "Wait," I called, "Jay"—though I was squinting at Jordan, whom I now made out in the shotgun seat, eyes shut and chin tilted back to point at the sky, the scarf covering her nose and mouth. "How do I reach you?" I yelled, though what I meant was, when might I see him, and this woman, again.

"Telephone me from the garage," Gatsby answered. He put the car in gear, and as the Rolls started to move away the woman turned her head, so that the scarf fell away from her mouth, and she looked at me with those slanted, wolf-colored eyes.

"Wha' don't you come to the party?" she called, one side of her mouth pitching the question, the other ready to catch what her words conveyed. "He throws one most every weekend, on the ah-land"; and Gatsby waved his straw hat in what I chose to interpret as agreement. Dust billowed; and the rats and I stared as Gatsby's rolling palace swerved onto the track, sped up, then plunged back into the dust and smoke of that underworld of ashes from which we earlier had emerged.

—

Sitting in the coffeeshop with Marcus Fayerweather a few hours later, I was happily conscious of the one-hundred-and-seventy-five dollars in my trousers pocket, an advance on my first week's wages; and my earlier wonder had settled into a less frenetic feeling of bemusement, tempered by sharp demands of a more practical nature. I was abominably hungry, for one thing, and the smell of chops that the restaurant's manager, a Greek named Mavromikalis—known, inevitably, as "Mike"—was grilling for someone else, brought the juices swirling 'round my tongue.

I was also acutely conscious of not having bathed since I left Duluth five days ago. I cringed to imagine what Jordan Baker must have thought of my aroma. The room Fayerweather had showed me—it was over the warehouse, next to his own—held only a tiny washstand, which was a let-down from my room at the Metropole. But Fayerweather told me the Greek would heat water, and I could borrow the tin bath and soap he used himself, as long as I did the bucket-work.

The bath, and food, could wait; the one thing I craved above everything else was a drink, and a drink stood before me, strong and cool in a chipped coffee cup.

I was beginning to like Marcus Fayerweather. He'd been in the Navy, as had I. He started out as medical orderly, then steward on a four-stack destroyer, and became a deckhand in the course of one Atlantic convoy in which three of its merchant ships were torpedoed. This meant we shared the dialect of wet steel, ropes and cold night watches marking a man as member of that saltwater fraternity. He liked to talk, and packed a lot of information into sentences that were numerous, if short.

One of my first questions, once we had repaired to the coffeeshop, had to do with Gatsby's relationship with Jordan Baker. Marcus had shaken his head and chuckled. "She's not his lady-friend," he said, "if that's what you're asking. That girl does not like the long-term. I hope you're listening?"

"I'm listening," I replied.

"Good. Most people don't. Fact is, he's got some other dame, out where he lives." He chuckled again. "Never guess her name."

"You're right," I said, staring at the grill where Mike was spooning mashed potatoes and gravy next to the chops, "I can't."

"Daisy," Marcus said. "That's the lady's name. Which is why the boat," he added unnecessarily. "And the man's plumb half-crazy about her, like the song says, the girl not the boat, but"—he shook his head again—"she's taken, or something. The dame, I mean. Anyway he can't even go near her, is what Miss Baker told me, he's so wound up about it all. *So* wound up."

We were drinking gin. It was very smooth, light and junipery compared to the rotgut Mrs. Virtanen served. Marcus had bought the first round, which endeared him further to me, though given how I was quaffing neat gin on an empty stomach I was liable, right now, to fall in love with anyone in sight. On this joint's menu, chalked up in surprisingly florid letters over the stove, the drink was called "English tea."

This "tea," Marcus said, was a bonus from the first and only run the *Daisy* had made so far, under a skipper who disappeared ten days later, for reasons Marcus would not go into. Instead of elaborating he looked away, through the window where there was nothing to see but a barren stretch of dusty roadway, a pair of train tracks, the loathsome creek, and the land of ashes smoking infernally on the far side—and rising above it all, on a high pillar that must have made them starkly visible to passengers on trains crossing the drawbridge, a pair of giant, weirdly hooded eyes that stared at you, in the manner of a Rembrandt portrait, from any angle you might choose.

The eyes, which existed by themselves, without a face, were framed by a pair of mustard-colored spectacles; all pasted fifty feet overhead on a massive billboard advertising an oculist whose name was printed in equally giant letters beneath: DR T.J. ECKLEBURG.

The billboard had faded and flaked from sunlight and the corrosion of soot. This, I saw now, was responsible for the hooded effect, as the billboard was rusted on or near the upper half of both retinas. Perhaps Dr. Eckleburg had paid for its erection a long time ago and then died, I thought, or moved away, leaving only his eyes to grimly watch over herds of people going to and from their jobs in the city. I was still watching them when a woman in a pleated skirt, high heels and pink blouse, wearing a large, sun-colored hat decorated with paper roses, banged through the doors of the coffeeshop.

She looked around the little joint as if she owned it. I was seated facing her and the first impression I got was one of heat—heat kindled by rage, or passion, or at least the kind of fiery curiosity that sometimes makes up for a lack of beauty. I don't mean to imply that she was ugly. Her face was round, and pretty enough, though not in the same category as Stella Wolfshiem or other women I'd seen in the city next-door; but she was plump and filled that blouse like stuffing filled a chicken. And her hands were small, with fingers fat

as sausages. Her eyes held mine for a good four or five seconds and
it was disconcerting, to say the least, to move from the giant hooded
peepers of Dr. T.J. Eckleburg to eyes far smaller but holding mine
with equal force. In my semi-inebriated state she resembled a Fury,
a fair and vengeful spirit come inexplicably to wreak her desires
upon the diner.

She looked then at Marcus, sniffed in disapproval and turned
to the Greek.

"A quick coffee, Mike. I'm taking the 7:20 to Penn Station."

Through the window beside me George Wilson hove into view,
lumbering in the woman's wake. He had driven us here in the flivver with the "for sale" sign, then disappeared into the garage where,
Marcus said, he lived with his wife. By the way she turned to glare
at him, hands on hips, when he entered the coffeeshop; by how he
edged up close to speak to her, it was clear this was the woman he
was married to.

"I was only askin' where you're going," he said. "Myrtle," he
added, as if to ensure she knew he was talking to her, or to affirm
some right attached to the process of naming.

"I don't have to tell *you*," she replied. Her voice was husky, tense.
"You tie me down to a dump like this, a dump where Negroes sit
with decent white folk any day of the week"—she flapped a pudgy
flipper in Marcus's direction. "An' you expect me to stay *here*, day in,
day out? Well, nuts to that."

"I don't mind." Though he had cleaned the smudge off his
forehead, Wilson still held a rag in one hand, maybe the same rag
he'd used on the *Daisy*. His voice held something of passion too, I
thought, but the tone of it was like a reverse image of his wife's; he
spoke in notes high and modulated where hers had gone deeper, and
low in trajectory as a thrown knife. "I just want to know when—I
mean, what time you're coming back."

They stared at each other for a few seconds. Something changed
in her: she put out a hand to touch him, then held it shy of his arm.
I saw him lean forward, just a degree or two, toward that hand

when he thought they might make contact, then lean back when they didn't.

"I told Cath we'd try to see a picture show, is all."

"So you'll be on the eleven-fifteen?"

"I'll be back when I fuckin' well *feel* like it," Myrtle snapped. Sweeping a last, defiant look around the coffeeshop, she stepped around her husband and out. The five men in that little place: myself, Marcus, the manager, a walk-in customer, and Wilson; watched her through the window as she stalked across the ash-paved roadway, then leftward along the train tracks toward Flushing, her pale, doughy arms pumping as she hurried. The coffeeshop seemed cooler, all of a sudden, as if she'd stolen some of the heat that powered the men within.

And Dr. T.J. Eckleburg watched with us as behind his billboard the setting sun, filtered by smoke and dust rising from the Land of Ashes, sank through lilac clouds: a disc of scarlet that Marcus eyed with resignation.

"Red sky at night, sailors' delight," he said softly. "But that's a damn lie, ain't it? 'cause the sky's always red in this place, and there isn't a ton of delight to be had here either."

Chapter Four

I spent the next four days on the *Daisy* with Marcus, getting to know the boat's gears and idiosyncrasies, as well as charts of the area I was supposed to navigate. Under lamps hung in the wheelhouse Marcus went over the controls, which were standard: compass and wheel for steering; fuel pumps, throttles, chokes and ignition for the engines. When we were at sea Marcus would double as engineer, Wilson not having signed on for sea duty. Another man—one of Wolfshiem's many relations, Marcus said—would work as deckhand.

The starboard engine was inoperative during my first week on the boat. Gatsby had decided to replace all jets, not just the defective one, on the engine's twin carburetors, and the parts were slow in arriving, which made the mechanic nervous. I wanted to move the *Daisy* out of its hiding place, on port and middle engines only, to get a feel for the craft and how it handled. But the rules Wolfshiem and Gatsby laid down, Marcus told me, precluded going out for any reason deemed non-essential—the only "essential" reasons being to refuel (but the boat's tanks were already full) and to test the starboard engine once it was repaired.

I didn't mind. The weather during those few days cooled somewhat. I still had not got used to working beside the ash-chute from Hell's boiler and already was developing a rough, if infrequent, cough due to breathing the dust that floated in through the boathouse's cracks. But for a while, at least, I took pleasure in returning to the one job I had truly trained for on *Tuolomee*, on the tugs and subchaser too. I pored over those charts, memorizing the shape of Long Island Sound, its depths and tides, all the way east to Shagwong Reef and Montauk—and beyond, to Block Island Sound, in case our rendezvous occurred further afield. I plotted provisional courses from the creek north to Flushing Bay and the eastern portion of the East River, through the twisting bottlenecks of Whitestone and Throg's Neck, City Island and Sands Point, into the more open waters of the Sound itself.

If the one run he'd done was any indication, Marcus Fayerweather said, we would be instructed to anchor at the tip of Young's Island in Stony Brook inlet, about a third of the way along Long Island's north shore, while waiting for the freighter to reach our mid-Sound rendezvous. Once the cargo was aboard we would speed south through Port Jefferson inlet to a dock in Setauket Harbor, where a crew would be waiting to load our cargo into trucks.

"It's not Rum Row," Marcus commented, pointing on our small-scale government chart to the other side of Long Island. "That's open ocean, so obviously a lot more space. But it's like Fifth Avenue in Christmas season out there, just a crowd of schooners 'n freighters lined up three miles out, waiting for the boats to come out and buy hootch. You know they even tack up signs in the rigging, with the price of whisky and gin? That way you can run down the row, looking for the best deal. The best deal …." He chuckled. "So, lots more space, but lots more Coast Guard. And rum pirates, too."

"Rum pirates?" I asked.

"Yeah." His mouth lifted in a smile, and Marcus shook his head at my naïveté. "They're what it sounds like: bootleggers who attack other bootleggers, steal their hootch—steal their hootch. But"—his finger tracked back over the island, indicating the Sound where we were to work—"there's less traffic on the North Shore, for hootch I mean, so less pirates. You get a lot of legal ships, if that's the word

I'm looking for. Which is not a bad thing. Not a bad thing ..."
(Marcus, I had noticed, often repeated the same phrase twice, for
emphasis.) "It's cover for us."

I walked parallel rulers across the chart, and compensated for
the slight currents to draw a course. I measured the distances carefully with brass dividers, and worked out time-to-target for various
speeds.

I asked Marcus again about the *Daisy*'s first skipper, but as
before he refused to explain the man's departure, saying only something had happened he wasn't supposed to talk about, and that was
that. "You're makin' good money," he said, "real good money, right?"
I agreed. "Well, that kind of jack means two things: One, there's
gonna be some risk involved. And two, whatever happens, you keep
your mouth shut."

I tried, as suggested, to get in touch with Gatsby or Jordan Baker
by telephone, but the only number Wilson had was Wolfshiem's. I
left a couple of messages with his secretary, Stella, who told me in a
voice as cool and unwelcoming as Lake Huron in January that she
would pass them along.

But I never got a call back, let alone an invitation to the parties
Jordan had mentioned. I told myself they must be busy, and I was
busy, and anyway there would be plenty of time. And I buried the
niggle of hurt, from Jay's ignoring me, in work.

I spent time in the *Daisy*'s engine room. Wilson didn't care for
my presence, but I reckoned I had to know something about the
boat's power, especially if he wasn't going to be aboard when we
needed it most. Even in the chiaroscuro of kerosene lamps those
engines were beautiful objects: like big, shiny metal birds, the
folded wings of their cylinders rising at a thirty-degree angle on
each side, their round heads and bodies tucked into the driveshaft
beneath. Though he came from Brooklyn originally, Wilson had
worked during the war at the Lincoln plant in Detroit which built
these engines; it was why Wolfshiem had hired him. When I asked
the mechanic about technical details he forgot to be confused and
talked freely, for him: going into the vacuum created by the Venturi

tube in the carburetors, bemoaning their tendency to gum up in maritime conditions—stuff I barely understood but to which I listened patiently, watching his bland, handsome face lose its acid pallor as he described his charges.

We ran the center and port engines twice—not for long, as the exhaust they created filled the boathouse with smoke so dark and thick it rivaled the Land of Ashes in toxicity, and immediately turned my low-grade cough from the ash fires into spasms so violent I could barely stand upright. The engines' noise was oddly high in register, and ear-splitting. (There was an underwater port for the exhaust to muffle noise during a run, but its valve was rusted shut.) I did not dare put the working V-12s in gear for more than a few seconds for fear of pulling down the rickety boathouse to which we were moored, but I could already tell that synchronizing three powerful engines to hold a straight course was going to be a problem.

It was just after the exhaust had cleared following one such test, while I was checking the bilges to make sure vibration had not opened any seams in the boat's light planking, that I heard a woman's voice. In this environment of men, smoke and machines, the delicacy and pitch of it felt like the first warm day after a long, hard Minnesota winter. Jordan, I thought, and climbed so quickly to the deck that I barked my left shin on a coaming. But the woman standing on the dock had black hair, whose curls joyfully escaped her hat.

"Stella," I said.

"Don't sound so disappointed, Mister Laine," Wolfshiem's secretary said. "I've come to take you away from all of this."

━

What Stella had really come for, it turned out, was to cure Wolfshiem's distaste for Jon Laine's clothes, a distaste that even I shared. I was not, as a rule, particularly conscious of fashion; but I was still aware of having only one hat and a couple of shirts to my name, along with the threadbare suit Wolfshiem had observed with such disdain—everything now soiled with ash and dust, sweat and engine oil.

Stella had a taxi waiting, which took us through the Land of Ashes, the driver complaining all the while. "I ain't never been here and I ain't never comin' back, you got no idea what this is doin' to my air filter," he whined, all the way to the train station in Flushing, where we caught a local to Penn Station. From there we hopped an elevated train downtown. Less than a week had passed since my last visit to Manhattan but I felt as overwhelmed as before, my brain a keyboard of raw senses banged on by enthusiastic if unskilled players: a ragtime of colors and noise, heat and people.

On 9th Street Stella led me to a department store fourteen stories high, an entire block in width. I'd heard of Wanamaker's before—it was famous for having a modern short-wave radio set on which news of the *Titanic* disaster had first been received—but I wasn't prepared for the scale or grandeur of this cathedral to commerce. Twin ceremonial staircases led from a crowded nave, lit by giant, wrought-iron candelabra, to floor upon floor of marble archways and glittering balconies through which one glimpsed a million manufactured eucharists—all the treasures of Christendom piled and worshipped, displayed and sold.

On one of those floors Stella marched up to a high priest of the cult, a man with nose so curved and eyes so beady he resembled a tall, dissipated turtle. His sparse hair was glued in precise rows to his scalp, and he was dressed in a harshly pressed suit with a watch fob chained to the waistcoat and a cerulean handkerchief in his breast pocket. Ranks of similar suits hung on polished walls behind him. The turtle refused to regard either me or Stella at first, and when she insisted I be fitted for three suits, one blue, one brown and one gray, to be charged to the account of Mr. Jay Gatsby, he answered her while looking at a point six inches to one side of her face, in a way she was probably used to from Wolfshiem.

When he did consider me, as he had to in order to fit the suits, the turtle's expression changed from reptilian indifference to one of outright disgust. But he measured me all the same, picking suits off racks and pinning in cuffs and pant legs, touching me only with the very tips of his fingers. "An excellent serge suit," he muttered bitterly. "Long fiber, pure wool worsted in houndstooth twill." He sounded close to tears. "Five-button vests, long soft rolled lapels, vented in back."

While the suits were being altered Stella and I walked the men's-wear chapel, in which shirts of every color and pattern lay piled so high on tables they appeared ready to topple; where a tribe of other well-dressed turtles assembled, on Stella's instructions, not only shirts but socks, ties, and a trio of hats. When the suits were ready she told me to change into one, and a new shirt, tie, hat and shoes as well. The shirt I put on felt soft and clean as a mother's touch; the shoes smelled wonderfully of calf's leather. When I came out of the dressing room Stella bade me look in the nearest mirror; and I felt strangely excited to see how the grimy boat skipper in a stained, worn jacket and greasy pants could be transformed, by a mere change of duds, into a person of elegance, even importance.

The face that looked back at me was the same: plain and square, with a broad nose and hazel eyes somewhat sunken beneath beige hair that continually and untidily swooned over a large forehead. The scar on my left cheek, from a childhood sledding accident, reinforced my recognition. I was still five-foot-eight, of course, with shoulders and feet disproportionately wide. But those feet were now shod in brogues of fine, deeply polished calfskin, while the working-man's figure had changed into something slimmer, perhaps even skilled at waltzing, with tapered waist and a silken tie. A felt Panama hat brought my forelock under control. A blue silk handkerchief, folded like the peak of a lateen sail, poked out of my blue breast pocket. The turtle came within a mere fathom of smiling as he contemplated the miracle he'd wrought. Even Stella seemed impressed; she did smile, with one corner of her mouth, and looked me up and down saying, "Well *well*, Mister Laine." Practically holding his beak, the turtle had folded my old clothes in a paper bag; and as we emerged from the cool, soft lights of Wanamaker's into the scorched streets, Stella walked over to a trash collector's cart and dropped it in, then wiped her fingers on her dress.

"Wait!" I yelled. The trash collector already had his hands on the bag to look inside. I grabbed it from him, took out the clothes. I pulled from the trousers my wad of wages, which I had buried in the side pocket of my pants; from the jacket I rescued a small, worn daguerreotype, which I slipped inside the breast pocket of my new jacket. The trash collector shook his head in contempt, and Stella asked mockingly, "That your girl?"

"It's private," I muttered.

Despite my rudeness she started talking then, as she had at the Metropole. Wolfshiem was sending her to Chicago next week, she said, to ferry contracts to his office there. I'd stopped to buy a blini from a street vendor, for the whole department-store experience had made me hungry; perhaps it was just Jon Laine's body instinctively seeking reassurance that despite the new suit he was still what he'd always been, a sailor from Minnesota with a taste for street snacks. She told me not to spill grease on my jacket, then asked for a blini as well and I bought her one, and we stood there eating the greasy, onion-stuffed pancakes, sweating in our fancy city clothes.

After, we both lit cigarettes and walked slowly toward the elevated train. "See how the girls are lookin' at you now?" she said, and it was true. People, and especially women, were eyeing me as they never had the last time I walked Manhattan's streets.

I told her that, in my experience from another life, girls looked at a fellow more freely when he walked with another girl, as if protected by the watchfulness of their own kind, and she said, "Maybe—but also, this morning they were figuring you for an apple-knocker; now they're not so sure."

Jordan Baker: her mobile mouth, the way she tilted her head back; had touched a spot inside me, a space near the middle of my chest that once was soft as moss and warm as July, a spot I'd thought long ago burned out. But now I found it could also take pleasure in walking the streets of New York with a girl as pretty and sharp as Stella; and when she glanced at me with her big, coal-colored eyes my heart-rate sped up a notch.

It was then I truly realized, and for the first time since leaving Duluth, that life could, indeed, get better—that hope, as Gatsby had always implied, was not a rare herb which showed up once in your life, if you were really, really lucky and turned over the right stone. It might also reveal itself to be a crop as lush, gilded and bountiful as all the wheatfields of Minnesota.

—

I had expected Stella to lead me back to the Flushing train at Penn Station but instead we got off the El at Times Square, where we found Wolfshiem smoking a cigar outside a corner restaurant at 49th Street and Broadway. He stood in the center of a tribe of men and didn't spot us until Stella waved at him over the shoulders of the crowd; a few minutes later he shook hands with some of the men, nodded at me, and headed for the restaurant.

"This is where I take a powder," Stella said, with that one-corner smile.

"Wait," I burst out. I was reluctant to see her go. As it had in the boathouse, her voice—high and light as blown leaves compared to the dog-grunts and roughness of males—felt like a gift I did not wish to return.

"I still," I said, groping for some way to hold her back if only for a few seconds, "I want to find some jazz joints, maybe we could meet later?" At which she frowned and said, "Are you asking me out, Mister Laine?" And when I stammered, "Oh no, not really, but it would, I mean maybe," she replied, "You got no idea where I come from, Mister Laine. My family would disown me, for a start. But it's nice of you to ask."

She turned away, then back. "I hear Edmond's Cellar, uptown," she called, and her frown was gone, and so was she—her small, black-clad body, the dark hat and curls, vanishing among the passersby as if diving back into some great human pool where you had to make a conscious effort to stay afloat.

The restaurant into which I followed Wolfshiem was brown. It had high brown ceilings, square tan columns, a long brown bar in back, and what looked like hundreds of tables, barely visible through an umber haze of tobacco smoke. The noise of plates and conversation was loud as a steam engine. A portly man in a coffee-colored suit bowed to Wolfshiem and led him, myself, and four of the men from outside through a traffic of slow diners and fast waiters to a corner in back. Wolfshiem took the table tightest to the angle and pointed me to the chair facing him. The other four fellows sat one each at the four tables surrounding. I noted now that every one of them bore the snide, watchful look I had seen before on the faces of scab enforcers, of Pinkerton men.

A waiter brought us coffee. One of Wolfshiem's companions asked him, "Can I have my usual?" and Wolfshiem replied, "Okay but make it quick, I gotta be on Hester by two. He loves the homemade cheese pie," Wolfshiem explained to me, or maybe to himself, and snapped his fingers at another of his companions, who produced a map from under his jacket and handed it to his boss.

Now Wolfshiem looked at me for the first time, or not at me exactly since he still looked at everything sideways, but at my new serge suit, my crisp new Panama hat. "Not bad, Mister Laine," he commented, "you might make a New Yorker yet." He stubbed out the stogie he'd been gnawing, lit another and, after giving our surroundings a quick once-over, opened the map on the table between us.

"I got word from Saint Pierre," he said, "the *Loch Alsh* left yesterday and it's doo off Montauk three days from now. They'll meet you here on that night"—he pointed to an "x" inked in not far from where Marcus had shown me. "I wrote down the latitude and longitude—you can do that, right?" I nodded. "It's basically a milk run, six miles doo north from Port Jefferson, almost as much from the Connecticut coast—'course the ship's gotta pass Fisher's Island first but the Feds won't be anywhere near…. And you'll offload inside that harbor, Port Jefferson—Fayerweather knows where."

"The starboard engine's still not fixed," I pointed out. "Wilson said it—"

"You got two other engines, right?" he interrupted. I nodded again. "Then you'll have to make the run on those two. You can do that, right?" I got the feeling that not only did Wolfshiem use that phrase a lot, it was also not a question, so I agreed. A fellow in a yellow suit and an oversized straw hat danced his way toward our tables, got a nod from one of the men surrounding us, and handed Wolfshiem another slip of paper. This Wolfshiem read, and blessed with a brown plume of smoke from his cigar. He pulled a watch from his waistcoat and glared at it.

"I gotta make a telephone call," he said, and looked near my face again. "You stay at the garage, starting tomorrow noon. Got that? Don't go anywhere. Someone will call you with the exact time an' code to meet the ship." He stood up, turned to leave, and his four companions stood up with him. The man who had ordered cheese pie complained, "I ain't got my order yet, Mister W.," and Wolfshiem replied, "Let junior here eat it, looks like he could use the extra grub."

Then he turned back toward me. "The pie is Lindy's specialty," he told my tie, or maybe my handkerchief. "It's ambrosial." He leaned closer.

"One more thing: Keep an eye out for anyone hanging around the garage that doesn't have business there, especially—" He shook his head. "Huh, it's not likely. But just—keep an eye out. If you see someone, or if Mike or any of the guys sees someone—you call me *immediately.*"

Wolfshiem cranked up his gaze to my chin to mark the importance of what he was saying. Then he and his men walked into the clash, steam and hubbub of the restaurant, from which a few minutes later a waiter emerged bearing a wedge of pale pie covered with syrupy scarlet strawberries; a dish that proved, as Wolfshiem had predicted, ambrosial.

—

The call came in, as Wolfshiem had also predicted, three days later, a few minutes before two in the afternoon. The *Loch Alsh* was off Block Island and heading into the Sound. Steaming at eight knots it would reach the rendezvous point around 10:30 p.m. The weather was fair and the trip from Flushing Creek, I had already figured, would take the *Daisy* a little over two hours at half speed.

We were to leave early and anchor in Stony Brook Inlet, just west of Port Jefferson, to wait. Once we reached the rendezvous point we should look for a green-colored lantern flashing two longs, one short, two longs; in return we would flash three shorts on our searchlight.

Wolfshiem's cousin had showed up that morning, driving a Studebaker Light-6 so old it backfired with the regularity of a gassy octogenarian. He was a kid of 19 or 20, named Young Sam, apparently to distinguish him from an older Sam whom we were never to meet. He had pimply skin and the puppy fat still on him. He talked a bit rudely, to mask his nervousness; this would be his first run. He wore a jacket too big for him and a hat too small, sweated gently, and looked around with clear interest while pretending to be bored by everything. He reminded me of myself at that age, so intent on appearing a man of the world that it only proved how callow I really was. Wilson was giving the *Daisy*'s working engines a last tune-up, so Young Sam drove me and Marcus to the creek; and forty minutes later Wilson tailed onto the chain that hauled the "gio ... & Sons" boathouse doors open, let go the dock lines; and I eased the *Daisy*, its two engines burbling like restive leopards, into Flushing Creek.

Oh and it was fine to feel the boat start to lift and roll as it turned into the sun-splashed carouse of the East River. I could tell, even riding high and free of cargo in one-foot waves, that *Daisy* was responsive to its rudder and moved easily through its natural element. I could also tell that, like a three-legged hound, with the starboard propeller idle the boat had a strong pull to the right. I sent Young Sam down to check with Marcus that the other two V-12s were working normally and then, once he confirmed, goosed their throttles to half power. The boat leaped forward, its bow and then the rest of the hull rising to glide on its shallow, flat bottom; surging so powerful and enthusiastic that I had to hold onto the wheel in order not to fall backwards—and Sam, now standing beside me, did stumble aft, yelling, "Hey, go easy!" But we grinned with shared excitement from the thrust and speed. Even at half power and with one engine dead, I had never gone so fast on water. We must have been moving at over twenty-five knots, and we passed tugs and ferries and an eastbound paddlewheeler as if they were pinned to rocks.

I kept watch through binoculars but, as Wolfshiem and Gatsby had promised, no Coast Guard or any other patrol boats came into view; though at Throg's Neck a low, dark-hulled launch with a rounded pilothouse in the middle of its considerable length pulled out from Little Neck bay on a course parallel to ours.

It did not look official and, remembering Marcus's words about "rum pirates"—remembering also Wolfshiem's warning about strangers hanging around—I checked with Marcus again, then opened up the engines to two-thirds power. And the *Daisy* picked up her skirts, lifted her bow half out of the water, then settled into a fast smooth hurtle, smacking down the higher waves as if to spurn them, leaving a high "V" of thrashed whitewater and the roar of twenty-four big cylinders in our wake.

As we entered the Sound proper we were moving at such speed that I had to twist away from the wheel every half-minute to refer to marks and course changes on the chart so as not to veer close to rocks and other obstructions on our run eastward, and within ten minutes the black launch had disappeared into a light heat-haze over the distant, frilled beaches of the Westchester islands.

———

Seven hours later we were idling under a star-salted night at the rendezvous point, rocking in dark, three-foot swells as we watched the shadow of a ship move slowly from the northeast in our direction. My heart was beating hard as I thought about all the things that could go wrong, not least the possibility that this steamer was not the *Loch Alsh* and would collide with us where we lay, also without lights, before we could move out of its path. The engines choked and grumbled impatiently as their exhaust ports dipped in and out of the swells. Marcus sat with me in the wheelhouse. Young Sam was busy throwing up, for the fourth or fifth time, over the side.

"You'd think Wolfshiem would find us someone who wasn't gonna be seasick," Marcus said, and then, "Flash the searchlight again, in case they didn't see us—they didn't see us."

I did as he suggested but the steamer did not respond. It was hard to see its shape, though it looked the right size for a Scottish coastal freighter. A pale moustache of bow wave indicated it was not slowing as it was supposed to. "The hull's not white," Marcus said, "and it's too big. It's not a cutter." Then the shadow narrowed, indicating the ship was turning. "She's coming toward us," Marcus said urgently, "we better get out of the way, it could be—" He didn't finish the sentence; he didn't have to. Suddenly the shape seemed much bigger than before.

I opened up the throttles and spun the wheel to starboard. "Get that Browning out?" I said to Marcus. "Just in case." But at that very second a bright green lamp flashed on the higher part of the ship's silhouette: two longs, one short, two longs. The shadow lengthened again as the freighter turned away to clear us. I flashed the required response, then maneuvered *Daisy* in a wide circle behind the ship to come up close on its port side. Illuminated by the slight starlight and a work lamp now shining on the ship's superstructure, the *Loch Alsh* reared above, a great wall of rust interspersed with patches of black paint and seaweed. It surged, gasping, sank and surged again, revealing a glisten of boot topping, a fringe of barnacles at the waterline.

"*Daisy?*" came a voice from above. "*Loch Alsh*," I called in reply, and Marcus and Young Sam threw lines to tie us in.

—

I have never worked so hard, at sea or on land, as I and my crew worked on that and similar nights. We were moored to the ship, fore, aft and in between, with bumpers out, but the *Loch Alsh* had to keep moving, albeit slowly, to maintain steerage way, and the *Daisy* kept banging into and out from the ship's rough side, causing me to wince internally as the two vessels rose and fell to swells at slightly different times. Meanwhile fifteen feet overhead the *Loch Alsh's* crew piled case upon wooden case of liquor, as well as the occasional oaken barrel, into a cargo net which they lowered on a tackle down the vessel's side for us to haul aboard.

Three men from the *Loch Alsh* climbed down a pilot ladder to help, bulky fellows with accents thick as porridge and hard to understand, but even with their help it was slow work. Every net-load held around forty cases which had to be carried by hand down a hatch between *Daisy's* two cabins, fire-ganged through the dim-lit space below, and stacked. The barrels had to be chocked, too.

Occasionally we spotted the lights of other ships moving through the night, and one of them came close, but none altered course toward us. Except for a couple of boats clearly fishing off Connecticut, no smaller craft appeared.

We finished loading around two in the morning. Marcus piloted us carefully through the Port Jefferson inlet; the government chart for that area held about as much information as a sketch of the Moon. We moved very slowly into an ebb tide, myself steering and checking the chart as Marcus called out bearings and Young Sam, who seemed to have had the seasickness cooked out of him by the burn of nerves and the effort of loading, stood lookout.

After only one missed turn and a slight scrape on sandy bottom, Young Sam spotted the green lantern marking the Setauket Bay dock Wolfshiem had indicated. The eastern sky was dreaming that a blue color might just be feasible by then. Six trucks and a dozen men were waiting as we tied up, and before the sun had heaved its flaming hulk over the horizon the *Daisy* was unloaded and we were leaving the inlet, dragging a wake stained pink with dawn as we made our way back into the open Sound.

Chapter Five

I slept like Rip van Winkle for several mornings after our run: the first morning to catch up on my sleepless night on Long Island Sound; and the following days because the run had worked and because Wolfshiem's cheese-pie man, who had been in charge of offloading, had paid off *Daisy*'s crew. I'd received the balance of my first week's salary plus a five-hundred-dollar bonus, all of which I kept rolled and tied with marline in the pocket of my new trousers. Of course I ranked far below the financial firmament of Gatsby and Wolfshiem, but this was the most money I had ever possessed at any one time and I felt like a millionaire who could afford to get up when he pleased and so slept late with pleasure and no guilt.

When I awoke I washed, put on my new gray suit, my new shoes, tie and hat, and ambled over to Mike's restaurant, where I ordered whatever I felt like and a bit more.

The only trouble was, I had nowhere else to spend my newfound riches. Wolfshiem, by phone to Wilson, had renewed his stand-by order: Marcus and I were to remain at the garage till further notice to await the second ship, whose departure date and thus arrival time were uncertain. Young Sam had disappeared in his farting Studey the morning after the run; presumably Wolfshiem would know how to summon him when the time came.

My first amazement at Manhattan's flash and flurry had not been dulled by the excursion with Stella—rather, it had turned into

a longing, less jagged perhaps but wider and deeper in strength, to
dive back into the city's excitement the way a kid might plunge into
a lake back home and, opening his mouth wide, let in water to taste
and even drink out of a pure joy in swimming.

The most particular channels of that longing had to do with
city women, and also my ongoing desire to hear music. In Duluth
there had been a few clubs and concert halls where new music was
performed, and Seppo Kumpunen, who got me the job on the tugs,
had also passed on to me his deep love of jazz. On several occasions
we had attended a club where Dixieland was played, and I liked
that; but the concert that had hooked my mind and rhythm centers
was performed by an all-black Chicago band. They played a different kind of jazz in which the rhythms were stretched and smoked
out of more staid, traditional patterns by a trumpeter whose skills
seemed so advanced as to make one suspect him of some Faustian
pact; and by a singer whose voice filled the small joint full of more
lust and adventure than could be handled by mere listening. People
danced, at that club, with or without a partner, until the flatfoots
shut it down....

But New York City was closed to me, for now at least. Even
with Marcus or Wilson standing phone watch I could not leave garage or boathouse for longer than an hour in case the call came. So I
spent time cleaning up the *Daisy*. The wooden bumpers separating
our boat from the *Loch Alsh* had scraped up the boat's neat gunwales
and white hull, and it took several afternoons of scraping, sanding,
varnishing and painting to restore the yacht-like trim that was our
rum-runner's disguise.

At other times I slept, or (more rarely) read in my tiny room over
the warehouse. I had made the place as comfortable as possible, but
the bed was narrow and lumpy and the daguerreotype I had tacked
beside the sink mirror had its usual effect on me, which was to float
sadness into the room whenever I glimpsed it. Anyway I had little
to read: just copies, usually a couple of days old, of the New York
Daily News or *Tribune*; and a dogeared edition of *The Meditations
of Marcus Aurelius, Book One*, which I had studied over and over

during my time at St. Olaf. A phrase from the *Meditations*: "Thou hast power over thine own mind, not outside events: understand this and thou wilt find strength," seemed particularly appropriate to my current situation, and in my frustration at being both rich and cooped-up I drew solace from it.

And in truth my situation, though far from exciting, was a long way from miserable. After all, ships and tugboats provide good training for boredom. Mike's restaurant became my canteen and casino, the nexus of my social life. It consisted of one long, undistinguished room, painted in old-mothwing, with six booths lined up against the windows, three on each side of the entrance, and a pinewood counter with grill and shelves and a storage room behind. Since it was situated in an out-of-the-way area of Queens it attracted few passersby. Pinned against the drawbridge and railroad tracks, the open sewer of the Flushing River, and the enduring dust-storm of the Land of Ashes, it was not apt to please even the few who happened on it from more beaten paths.

This did not matter much to Mavromikalis since the chief purpose of his restaurant was to serve as front for the Wolfshiem/ Gatsby operation and he drew a wage for running it. The other buildings played different roles in the operation, as base for *Daisy*'s crew of course; they served as depot, also, for a different bootlegging activity of Wolfshiem's, about which I knew little, but that regularly used the warehouse underneath my lodgings. "You are only the rich part of their beez-ness," Mike told me, "you bring in tiger-milk, like this"—from under the counter he showed me the bottles, Gilbey's gin and Haig whisky, that he'd said came in on the *Daisy*'s first run. "This stuff, it go to Plaza Hotel, Delmonico restaurant, to all these rich fellows, *oi leftádes*, Gatsby find: that is his game. But after you, the ship, it take twenny-thousand bottles of cheap hootch to Rum Row, for *o laos*—for Wolfshiem people to run to his drug-stores … I should not confess this to you." He wiped his face with an apron.

Mike's English was not of the best but it was colorful in its braiding of Greek inflections and New York slang. The food he served was, if not great, at least edible. He liked to talk as he cooked

and cleaned, wiping his hand reflexively on his apron, wiping harder
when he got excited. Mike was a short man with a long nose, fat
black eyebrows, a lazy eye and a limp. He had his own philosophy
of life on which he based his judgments: a medley, as far as I could
tell, of folk sayings, poker, and a profound hatred of Turks, who at
the time were waging war against a Greek army in Asia Minor. "All
of eternity Ottomans think they are the bosses of Greece; now they
attack Greek cities in the east," he told me, decimating hash with
a spatula as, presumably, he would decimate the Turkish army had
he the chance. "This Mustafa Kemal says he is modern republic guy
but all he want is same as sultans, they want to glom *Hellas!*" The
hash, by this time, was half-burned …

Almost a week after our run Wilson received the parts needed
to fix the starboard engine. It cost him a morning to install them.
We took the *Daisy* from its hiding place that afternoon and tested
the repaired engine by running to a Port Washington boatyard to
refill our fuel tanks. As I'd suspected, getting all three engines to
spin at the right revolutions to keep *Daisy* moving in a straight line
was as easy as getting three cats to square-dance; but the speed we
achieved when all three V-12s were roaring at half-speed was even
more thrilling than when I'd pushed the throttles on our first run
eastward.

After that Wilson spent more time with our little group of regulars at Mike's, largely because the Greek, Marcus, and a couple
of local men who knew about it kept a game of poker cooking,
more as entertainment than for real gambling, at the farthest booth
from the door. One of the regulars was a low-rent con artist from
Astoria who had taken Wilson for eighteen dollars in four rounds
of thimblerig till Mike spotted what was going on and told him to
beat it—only to learn the con-man, like Mike, came from Kalamata.
From then on Stavros was allowed in on the poker games as long as
he never shuffled or dealt.

The stakes in our games were never high, but Wilson was a
hopeless gambler who could not refrain from playing when he
had time to kill. As far as I could tell his only other interest, apart

from Myrtle, was the "Gasoline Alley" comic strip in the *Daily News,* which sent him into high giggles every time he read it. He lost his shirt, over and over, at professional gambling tables; he was not bad at ranking the odds but when the pressure was on he was given to outrageous bluffs and no-roof bets that often as not cleaned him out and deprived him of a portion, or more, of the next week's salary.

Marcus had spent half his time on destroyers playing cards; and I'd learned the dark arts of poker on the tugs, so I could hold my own. But Mike was an artist at the game and won more often than not. He would refill the coffee pot, close the grill vents, hitch up his apron and sit in a chair drawn up to the booth, spine straight as a piling, watching the other players. His normally expressive face went quiet, the lazy eye shut halfway, and his eyebrows tightened to a slight frown. "*Kala,*" he would murmur when he won a hand, and rake in the coins with long, tobacco-stained fingers that invariably nursed a fuming cigarette.

Whereas Wilson's face, the rare times he won, would rise out of its usual shuttered confusion like a gray heron bursting from marsh grass, and how he smiled then was infectious and fine. Most of the time, though, he looked not only bemused but slightly sad, and when he lost a hand you would have thought all of New York's woes had melted into a mask of invisible lead to weigh his features down.

"It iss that broad Myrtle," Mike said one afternoon after Wilson had shambled back to his garage, having for once lost only a couple of dollars. Opening the restaurant's back door, he spat outside. "She give him trouble now like always." When I asked what kind of trouble—I was not much given to gossip (and there was something in Marcus Aurelius, the words of which I could not recall at the time, that was quite firm on the subject)—the thick eyebrows pulled together and Mike merely shook his head, repeating, "trouble." Marcus was at our table as usual, and he just looked at me and said nothing; though I could tell, from his lack of further expression, that he was of the same mind as Mike.

Occasionally Myrtle Wilson joined us in the restaurant and, unlike the first time I'd seen her, she was often gay and active,

constantly moving or fiddling around in a way that, curiously, reminded me of Gatsby. When she came in happy she made her
husband beam as if he'd won a hand, even though he hadn't. Her
plump face came alive and acquired beauty as she talked—as she
leaned forward, moving her upper body to the beat of her words,
her full breasts following a half beat behind.

One day in particular stuck in my mind from that period.
She had just picked up a women's magazine from a news-stand
in Corona. Mike, Marcus, Wilson and I were sitting at our usual
booth, drinking coffee with a shot of Haig's. Marcus and I had just
finished lunch and our plates lay around the table, making poker
impracticable for once. She banged through the door and observed
us, frowning slightly at Marcus's presence among white folk. But
she sat down with us anyway, beside her husband, which happened
to be as far away from Marcus as she could get, and spread the
magazine—it was called *Town Tattle*—in front of Wilson's not
insubstantial gut.

"Look," she said breathlessly, "isn't that fine?" Her pudgy fingers, tipped with crimson nails, stroked an illustration showing a
woman in a silken evening dress that draped her in folds like a
theater curtain's. "I bet I could make that, couldn't I, George?"

Wilson's smile expanded and he said, "I bet you could, Myrtle.
I bet you could."

"I only need to buy the cloth," she said, and nudged him playfully. "Whadya say, you ole cheapskate?

"I used to do a lot of sewing, when I was a girl," Myrtle continued, glancing at me and Mike while flipping the magazine's pages
back and forth. Now her eyes, her whole face seemed to glow, as if
her insides were heating up in pleasant ways, though it was already
hot in the little restaurant and the ceiling fans' chief job was to give
the flies a ride. Her eyes lost focus a little.

"I used to make gowns good as you'd find at Bergdorf's," she said
softly, "and I sold 'em too. But what I dreamed of was, I dreamed *I*
would go dancing in 'em, in some swell ballroom with an orchestra
and everything. You don't live forever," she added, looking around
for approval, "right?

"Then I met him." Her eyes were on Wilson now; she was still smiling but the glow in her had dimmed. "Seriously, George, I wanna make this. Seven bucks, I figure, for the silk. If you don't give me the money I'll find someone who will.

"So don't clean him out this time, fellas," she added, addressing everyone except Marcus with an expression that only pretended to threaten, and threatened all the same.

She left then, and once more it felt as if a source of great warmth had gone with her, abandoning the restaurant and the men in it to the kind of lassitude that pervades us when we are reduced to the usual, eternal and predictable vocations that men pursue in the absence of a woman to give it all a point.

Wilson left a few minutes afterward; we saw him later, sitting in the garage doorway, waiting for her to come home. Mike took our plates to the sink and threw them in. Crockery smashed. "*Gamoto!*" he yelled, and came back to our table, twisting the apron in his hands, leaning toward the window to peer down the ash trail leading to the garage. "She will get more green for that dress, you will see, she will call her fancy man."

"You best be quiet about that," Marcus told him, glancing at me. "Best be quiet."

"But she make George a *koroido*. How is it you say? Fool? Sucker?"

"Sucker?" Marcus said softly. "Sucker."

"Yes, sucker. It is not right."

"Everyone's got the right to live their life, an' how they choose to do that," Marcus said. "Long as no one gets hurt, it's no concern of ours."

"But she *will* hurt him," Mike said, twisting his hands even more angrily in his apron. "That man, she goes dizzy for him, but he is a friend to our bosses, if George he find out it will go very bad. In Greece we say, 'How you make your bed is how you will sleep'." He shook his head, looked at me. "You will see how she will sleep."

The last part of Mike's statement, at least, proved correct. A little after noon two days later I was staring out of my room's one window when the drawbridge horn sounded. The attendant waved from his little box and the bridge's span began to lift, slow as a snake's head in the sun. A minute later the 12:05 from Long Island wheezed and chundered to a stop, mumbling steam-dreams to itself as a tug with two ash-laden barges maneuvered toward the cut's dead water. A large man in a city suit, with blond hair fringing his boater, descended from the train and vaulted the low, whitewashed fence separating our ashen road from the tracks. He was followed by a second man, smaller and nondescript, also in a suit; he followed the blond man into Wilson's garage.

Shortly the two reemerged. The nondescript man—I never did get a good look at him—returned to the train, while the big blond fellow ambled down the road, just far enough to be invisible from the garage door. There he stopped, and lit a cigarette.

A minute later Myrtle came out of the garage, looked up and down the road, and approached him. The two did not embrace, but talked animatedly and close; then Myrtle returned to the garage, and the blond man followed his companion toward the train, walking calmly and slowly for the bridge was still up and only the tug had gone through. I saw him board the second car from the locomotive.

It was neatly done. Just as he disappeared Myrtle came out of the garage again, wearing a flowered hat this time, and bearing a little purse. Moving quite a bit faster than her friend, she hiked up her skirt, clambered over the fence, and made her way to the train, where a conductor in the last car opened the door for her and helped Myrtle aboard.

—

I took to walking, though not very far since Wilson insisted I obey Wolfshiem's one-hour rule. There was a saloon on Flushing Main Street where I sometimes drank a beer. A shop on the same street sold shiny new Victor phonographs; but though my newfound dough was throbbing for attention in my pocket, the shop's selection of records was so sparse—and it carried no jazz—that I did not buy the machine.

Often I would stroll up Kissena Boulevard to a hill from which I could see the towers and bridges of Manhattan shimmering in the hazy distance, as cool and unattainable as the cliffs of Thule.

And one afternoon, in a fashion that both harmonized with and was a function of everything Jay Gatsby had come to represent in my constricted world, everything changed—in the shape of a red flivver that swerved much too fast into the garage's gray forecourt, nearly hitting the pump and coming to an abrupt halt in a whirl-wind of mouse-colored dust and a small cry from its driver and sole occupant. And Jordan Baker got out.

I was at Mike's, as usual; playing poker, as usual, with Mavromikalis, Marcus, Wilson and a regular participant from Flushing. I was four dollars down in a hand of five-card stud (aces high, one-eyed jack wild) when I saw her walk into the garage. Wilson was in the hole, it was a normal game. For once I was glad to be losing too, since we could both leave the table without in-fringing the honor code of poker.

My pulse was galloping. I had dreamed of seeing Jordan for her own sake—which is to say for the sake of how, leaning her taut body back in that way she had, she looked at me from a position I'd read as both challenge and invitation. But lately she, and Gatsby too, had come to represent my sole, shining chance to escape the monotony of life at the garage, at the diner, and this added far more proof to the brew.

We found Jordan sitting in Wilson's filthy office, surrounded by chunks of oily machinery, spiked receipts, and dog-eared engine manuals. She was dealing five- and ten-dollar notes into piles. She glanced at me coolly as I followed Wilson in, and talked only to the mechanic, who stood awkward next to his desk while she relayed messages from New York. These were mostly about the warehouse which now, like the boathouse, required two shifts of guards to pro-tect a shipment that would be trucked in two nights hence from a place called Patchogue. The extra piles of cash were to pay the guards.

Then she asked me to shut the door. Even in the poor light from Wilson's desk lamp her way of sitting with head tilted back made her gray eyes glint as she flung that curveball smile; I thought her then the most attractive woman I had ever seen.

"Seems some fellows from Sicily want to take over the bootlegging in Queens, and Meyer says they're kahnda dangerous." The words rolled from her tongue in an unstable mixture of Southern drawl and unholy glee. This was all a big joke to her, I realized suddenly. I wondered then why Gatsby had got Jordan involved, and if she got much out of it besides entertainment.

"Jay an' Meyer say y'all have to keep more of a lookout, boys. Especially"—she paused for effect—"'specially for this one little Italian, named Mineo. Always wears a dark coat, even when it's hot"—she looked away and back, recalling what she'd been told—"has a round, fat face and eyes like this." She half-dropped her eyelids, but since her head naturally tilted back she didn't have to bend further in order to watch us. Her look reminded me of something I could not immediately place. "See? Bedroom eyes, Jay calls 'em"; and she laughed, too loudly.

"Coat's to hahd his gun," she continued. "If that guy comes hanging around, y'all call Meyer on the telephone toot sweet."

I followed her outside when she left.

"I tried to 'phone you," I said, "as you suggested, I—I left messages with Wolfshiem's secretary."

"Ah know," she said, and turned to face me. We had reached her car. "Ah'm sorry, but I had a golf tournament—I'm a golfer—didn't Jay tell you?"

"I haven't spoken to him, either."

"It doesn't matter." She put a hand on my arm and I almost shuddered, as if shocked by an electric wire. "Ah do have another life, besides Jay's and Meyer's shenanigans. In fact—"

She paused, and her smile deepened slightly. "Ah'm not usually 'llowed to come here at all, but Jay wanted me to, so I could ask you over to his place.

"Tonight," she added, "it's one of Jay's parties"—she pulled her hand away, and used it to point at the train tracks. "You take the local to West Egg, his drahver will pick you up."

"But I'm not supposed to—"

"Oh lordy, Jay *wants* to see you. It's his way of apologizing." She got in the car. "He'll square it with Meyer." The engine sputtered. She put it into gear and stalled, tried again, and this time got the flivver moving.

I watched her spin her own small tornado of soot as she sped down our track toward Flushing Main Street, under the permanent atmosphere of dust rolling east from the Land of Ashes; under the overarching gaze of the giant, blue and hooded eyes of Dr. T.J. Eckleburg, which I now realized had been in my mind ever since Jordan mimicked the Italian with the hooded gaze—as if we'd already been under observation, in some gearing that fate wound in by which the city and Italians from Sicily and the way things always worked in New York had been keeping tabs on our lives through those great, faded eyes since long before any of us even got here.

Chapter Six

T he train from Flushing required but half an hour and a dozen stops and level crossings to transport me from one world to another.

I got off at West Egg station in the honeysuckled quiet of a summer evening. Whereas Queens, even after sunset, baked in the heat stored in its asphalt streets and brick rowhouses, in West Egg jungled oaks and maples had sheltered the line from July's sun, and the air was cool and smelled of cut grass.

A crowd of cowed, besuited creatures, all bearing briefcases, vanished magically into waiting taxis, leaving a handful of men and women in more colorful dress to cast about the platform for guidance; which was eventually supplied by a chauffeur in livery of robin's-egg blue who beckoned from a station wagon the color of dandelions. The name "Gatsby" floated in the air, and I joined them. The car carried us through the sweet peach dusk, past a deserted high street, cottages and occasional glimpses of water, to the gates and granite postern of a large estate, and down an endless drive the postern guarded.

A great manor rose before us, its many windows and acres of surrounding garden pulsing with myriad colored lights, which an army of fireflies just beyond their reach sought to emulate in off-beat counterpoint. A hum of music and chatter meshed softly with the rhyme of tree frogs and crickets on the grounds.

I had dressed in the blue suit Stella chose for me at Wanamaker's, which I never used for work. With carefully shaved cheeks, polished shoes and the fedora-style hat, I seemed to have passed muster with my companions in the station wagon; and I thought I did not look much different from the other men already clustered around or under tents sheltering a regiment of linen-covered tables, and several outdoor bars.

At one such bar stood a group of thin, hungry-looking young men with accents so English and nasal they sounded as if each syllable might wander away if not lassoed by a sneer.

They were discussing a woman named Myra. "Two oilfields," one said.

"At least four, old boy," said another.

"I'd settle for one," a third put in. "More than enough to be getting on with, I should think."

When I asked the bartender for a gin he answered in a language so mysterious I fancied for a second it constituted another code to which I did not hold the key. "Fallen Angel, Clover Club, French 75, Ward Eight, Southside, Bee's Knees." One of the Englishmen, perhaps sensing my confusion, kindly suggested, "Try the French 75, it's the best this side of the Somme." Upon hearing this, the bartender ostentatiously hoisted a bottle of Gilbey's, poured a generous measure, added various elixirs. He thrashed the mixture in a shaker, dumped in something fizzy, and handed the foaming result to me in a thin glass, with an even thinner bow.

I walked the grounds, sipping the cocktail, which was tasty, if too sweet.

The house was even bigger than it had appeared at first. It was three stories high, built of stone in the style of a French château; mansard-strewn, ivy-freckled, laced with colonnades and porches, it would take several minutes of country walking to measure its length. A tower with a pointed top rose high over one end, and multiple terraces led, after a half-mile or so of white roses, yellow jonquils, emerald lawns, pink cabanas, and a marble swimming pool, to the smoked-blue rule of Long Island Sound, and a beach and dock attended by a raft and a pair of small motorboats.

Across the small bay, on another dock, a bright green lantern shone through the gathering dusk: symbol, I wondered, or fallback for Gatsby's rum-running activities? Though a man who would not show his face or phaeton at Wilson's garage for fear of being linked to our operation would surely not allow his cargoes to be smuggled where he lived, green light or no green light.

But I recognized the bay from *Daisy's* chart. It lay near-halfway between Flushing River and where we anchored in Stony Brook inlet to await our rendezvous. The combination of a mariner's contentment at knowing his position and the effects of the French 75, which I was now realizing had quite a kick to it, combined to put me in a mood that expected nothing but a general improvement in the fortunes of both myself and the universe as I went back to the tents to locate Jordan, and our host.

It took me a long time. I required two more French 75s to fuel my efforts. The drinks, working on an empty stomach, seemed to impart an unhabitual grace to my movements as I jinked and folded in and out of groups of guests, of dining tables. The girls here wore hair shorter and skirts higher even than in Manhattan, and seemed uniformly fresh and desperate, providing Jordan with a cover I found hard to pierce. Some swayed by themselves to a full orchestra on a canvas-covered floor under a tent that could have sheltered half of Finn Town, while a few couples twirled to Fox Trot tunes. More and more people appeared on the surrounding lawns. Here and there couples embraced at the very edge of light. I realized vaguely I had been among the earliest to arrive.

Suddenly hungry, and conscious that my swerves and promenades were starting to include unexpected loops attributable to gin, I sat at one table long enough to be served a plate of prawns in aspic, deviled eggs, and spiced ham. I carried the plate to a stone wall, half covered by beach roses, to eat; and it was there Jordan Baker found me with my mouth full.

"I've been looking all over for you," she said.

"Erm," I mumbled through aspic.

"Why don't you sit with us? I'll introduce you to some friends of mahn."

I put down my plate and she led me to a table a mere quarter-mile away, where two girls in yellow dresses and French bobs sat with a trio of men, everyone's faces polished and gentled by the flame of a glass-ensconced candle amid cocktail ware. Introductions were made. Someone talked in bitter tones about a play on Broadway. I didn't pay much attention, till I realized the conversation had shifted to Gatsby.

"I don't believe he exists," one of the women was saying, and the other nodded excitedly and said, "This is the third of his parties I've been to and I've not laid eyes on him yet."

"He's in hiding," the man next to her said confidently. "He was a German agent during the war, and when he killed a man—"

"Oh that's just a story," the first woman said. "I heard it from a lawyer in New York who knows him, he lives on a yacht that anchors all over." I could feel rather than hear Jordan trying not to laugh beside me. A man on my other side, dressed entirely in white flannel, said, "I can tell you he exists, and he lives here, 'cause I live next-door and I've seen him many—" at which point Jordan interrupted him, exclaiming, "Oh lordy, Nick, don't be so boring, the stories are *so* much better."

I was reminded, listening to this twaddle, of what Marcus had said about other people's affairs; and of the lines from the other Marcus, from the *Meditations*, he'd reminded me of. Only this time, despite my inebriation or maybe because I was drunk, I remembered the lines themselves:

"From my governor I learned … to work with mine own hands, and not to meddle with the affairs of others, and not be ready to listen to slander."

On a normal day I appreciated the *Meditations'* cool wisdom and simple cadence but tonight the lines seemed stale, prissy rather than profound, and I found myself agreeing with Jordan. Amid the soft lights, the swell and lick of music, the flocks of elegant men and pretty women; beside Jordan, who had sought me out and whose lean, tanned forearm rested only an inch from mine; and given the sense, it must be said, that the former Jaan Laine, ship's mate and tugboatman from Duluth, had just been admitted to a higher order of life distinguished by fine food, imported liquor, and educated company, a promotion he in some way surely deserved; the thrill of mystery, whether fabricated or not, seemed to outweigh any footling notions of morality or truth.

Or perhaps my knowing the truth behind these mysteries imparted such wisdom and resultant power that the gossip of the uninformed seemed, as a result, amusing and free of harm. I had found it, I thought happily, draining the last sweet drops of my latest French 75: the great dream of America, a dream Jay in some sense had always understood—that you could come from nothing and through wits and sheer persistence reach heights of power and scintillating luxury that others could only observe from afar—

The man in white flannel interrupted my thoughts. "At least," he said, leaning closer to me than was comfortable, "I've seen someone I *thought* was him." He looked around with a quarter-smirk, as if expecting to be surprised, and vaguely disappointed that he was not.

I glanced at Jordan, who was looking at the flannel man with a little frown on her face. Then she saw me watching her, and smiled her fast-ball smile. She was dressed in a white cloche hat and a long ivory dress that clung conscientiously to her breasts and hips; a silk scarf was wound loosely around her neck. I thought she looked both hugely desirable, and desperately unattainable, and the blend of contradictory feelings reawakened thirst in me. My glass stood empty and I told Jordan I was going in search of another. I offered to get a cocktail for her as well, but she simply held up her half-filled glass, and said something to the flannel man.

I got lost for a while after refueling. The property seemed to have taken on another one or two hundred dining tables, squadrons of girls in tight dresses, legions of white-suited men. A woman in a purple gown inquired of me, "Have you seen my tiara?" and glared when I said no. There was still no sign of Jay. I refueled again. I asked a few people at random if they knew where I might find our host, and they stared at me as if I had lost my mind and shook their heads or ignored me.

Suddenly tired, and in that stage of drunkenness where the world starts to let go its lines and drift in a seaway, I sat down at an empty table, watching servants dressed in black and white dump plates still heavy with aspic, potato salad, grilled steak, poached salmon into rolling rubbish carts. Slightly nauseated by the sight of all that half-consumed food, I closed my eyes to rest.

I must have fallen asleep because when I awoke most of the guests had gone. As if it had been waiting for a more intimate affair, a crescent moon now rose, shyly, against a cobalt sky to the southwest. By the moon's angle to the trees I knew it was late, or rather early the next morning. I wondered how I was going to get back to the garage, the last train having surely departed hours ago. My head ached savagely and I had a ferocious thirst. I got to my feet and walked toward the tents. Behind an unmanned bar I found a pitcher of water which I drained in long draughts. Then I poured myself a glass of champagne from an opened bottle, and for the first time entered the château.

There were still people inside. A couple danced in a vast sitting room in the shadow of a Roman bust perched on a column. The orchestra had packed up but someone far away played a piano. From a direction I couldn't place, as from some dimension of spirit, I heard the voice of the purple-gowned woman asking, "Have *you* seen my tiara?"

"You are not my husband," a woman in red told a man in beige, to which the man replied, "I was, I think, until an hour ago, and with the right blanshid—*blan-dishments*—I could be persuaded."

In a huge salon I found the piano player tinkling ragtime to a regiment of mirrors that would have pleased Louis XIV. Leaving him behind, I passed a telephone nook containing a small desk and velvet chair. The mechanism displayed its number: Egg Landing 153. I repeated it to myself, over and over, to hold it in memory despite the liquor.

When I finally made my way to the front door—down leagues of hallways, past dozens of French windows ducking behind curtains through which the sea breeze lethargically sighed; past a

Gothic library in which a chubby man in thick glasses sprawled on the carpet, crying in amazement, "Real books! *Real* books!"—I found Jay Gatsby and Jordan Baker, one on each side of the vast entrance, smoking and quietly talking.

"Ah do believe that dog will not hunt," Jordan was saying, "you'll have to find a different way now," and for an inebriated instant I thought they were actually discussing a blood sport.

It was warm, even in the foyer, but Gatsby looked as cool and unruffled as if he had just risen on a fresh May morning. He wore a yellow suit with a rose handkerchief in its breast pocket, and a light-blue shirt, striped in coral; and he stood with his usual grace, one foot in perfect spats hooked casually over the other, the finger of his left hand tapping on a silver cigarette case held in his right. The rush of happiness that overcame me when I saw him was, no doubt, due partly to the facility of emotion that gin conveyed. But it was also caboose to a long train of friendship, however jostled by time and different experiences, that I had become conscious of again upon seeing him in New York, and which I had subsequently—and I now sensed, deeply—missed.

"There you are, old sport!" he cried upon spotting me. "We were about to send out a search party."

I told them I had fallen asleep. As if we had parted only a few minutes ago Jordan wiggled her empty cup and said, "Ah'll take that drink now." Jay led us through a different set of corridors and French windows to a long inside bar fitted with stools in the shape of swans, where he poured amber slugs of Haig into a pair of glasses.

"It's thanks to Jon's skill you can drink this," he announced, lifting the bottle and smiling at me. "Here's to the good old days—that of course we may not mention—the voyage of the brave *Tuolomee*." His smile had the usual effect. On top of having newly discovered my birthright of opulent environs and the company of the rich and elegant, I was also the most interesting and important man in this house, perhaps in the entire New York area.

"I'm sorry it took me so long to bring you here, Jon," Gatsby continued, strolling to yet another French door through which, far away, I saw the bay emitting a visual purr under the brindled strokes of moonlight. The green light I'd noticed earlier sparkled beyond.

"Ah lost my scarf," Jordan complained, "ah'm *always* losing that scarf." Gatsby ignored her.

"I've been a bit snowed under, old sport," he continued, and his hands moved in that restless, wrist-less motion I remembered so well. "Snowed under with, ah, various businesses, of various kinds."

Then he strode through the door, and Jordan followed him, and I followed her. Before we had reached the jamb she swiveled, as fast as if she were initiating a Fox Trot. Looking at me in her usual way, as if to peer through invisible bifocals, she winked.

"He means Daisy," she whispered. I had not appreciably sobered up: this time it would take me minutes before I realized she was talking about something, or rather someone, very different from my rum-runner.

Jordan and I walked on together, joining Gatsby on a set of marble steps. We continued across a lawn, and a half-mile of terraces planted with day lilies, black-eyed susans, kiss-me-at-the-gate. People in black-and-white uniforms were still collecting tipped glasses and ravaged plates among the melted candles. A woman's shoe lay on its side by the pool, a man's tie adorned a stand of rosa rugosa, an actual girl sprawled unconscious on a chaise longue. Jay took Jordan's arm, and she took mine. As if drawn by the shine of moon, and the light of the lantern beyond, we walked together toward the bay.

French 75

ingredients

1 ounce gin
3/4 ounce fresh lemon juice, strained
half-ounce simple syrup*
4 ounces chilled Champagne

instructions

In a mixing tin combine everything except Champagne.
Add ice, shake well to chill. Strain into chilled flute glass
and top with Champagne. Garnish with a twist of lemon zest.
Serve immediately

*simple syrup: combine white sugar and boiling water
in a 1:1 ratio. Can be stored, refrigerated, for a week

Chapter Seven

My hangover from Gatsby's party immobilized me the next day and seemed to cloud my view of the world for a couple more days afterward. It was worse than any I remembered from Finn Town and from this I deduced that, with the exception of my night in West Egg, I had been imbibing less alcohol since I got to New York and had grown less inured to its venomous after-effects.

This, I supposed, was a good thing. At least Gatsby, who never drank, and the people who had brought us the Volstead Act would have said as much. And I reflected in sour amusement on the irony of a professional rum-runner paying respect, however transient, to the creed of teetotalers and do-gooders.

It also crossed my mind that many of my former comrades in the Finnish Socialist Federation, which supported temperance because of the often self-destructive love that Finnish workers nurtured for vodka, would have observed my miserable state and indicated, with a wordless shake of the head, "I told you so."

Even after the post-hangover wore off, the world I lived in seemed to have lost some of its previous lightness and wild spirit. I suppose the contrast between my daily environment and the glitter and thrill of Jay's festivities had a lot to do with it. The cough I'd developed from breathing the local miasma of ash dust and wind had worsened, probably because of all the cigarettes I'd smoked while drinking French 75s.

The weather didn't help. The temperature had wobbled for a week around the level of extremely warm and now clambered back to the thermometer's attic, and the humidity rose with it. One day clouds black as bruise and taut as a blacksmith's bicep blew in. Heat lightning cracked the sky, and the city was plunged into a half-darkness; but while dump dogs cowered, and all Queens held its breath in anticipation, little or no rain fell to bring its inhabitants relief.

I'd hoped Jordan would stop by the garage again although she'd implied that, like Gatsby and Wolfshiem, she was supposed to keep her distance from the sharp end of the operation. I thought she or Jay might telephone at least, given how we had all enjoyed each other's company at West Egg, but the only messages relayed to me by Wilson were updates on the *Loch Nevis*, still waiting for cargo off Newfoundland.

I found my spirits so low that I began to miss Duluth, where I had family at least, though what befell the Laines there had made it near-impossible for us to frequent each other. I thought of calling Uncle Tai to ask for news of my parents but somehow never crossed the line between uncertainty and resolve to book a line to Minnesota.

What saved me, in those heat-stunned days and nights, was talking to, and sharing stories with, my crewmates.

It reminded me of the Navy. With nothing to do while drifting around with other subchasers looking for Austrian submarines in the Adriatic, the men on *SC 179* used to draw on things they had done or seen (and often enough things they had not seen but would happily lie about) to pass the time.

You have to remember I was a Finn, brought up to endure life in relative silence; it was because of this I found myself more fascinated than most with the telling of stories. I thought then—and still believe, despite all the harm such tales were to visit on Gatsby and those who knew him—that in this pursuit my shipmates both underscored and represented the true distilled spirit of humankind, which is to spin yarns to each other in order to learn how people cope with a life often beset by grief as well as boredom; a life that will end, all too soon, in an uncompromising void.

In this art, among all our group, Marcus Fayerweather was probably the more skilled, his stories the most engaging and apparently true. Some of them reached far back: memories of being raised as the youngest son of small-farmers in Mississippi, who moved to New York when he was twelve. What he recounted of life down South, of white foremen and vigilantes, of black boys hanged for looking twice at a white girl, got me thinking that the 19th Century had not yet ended in America. And I wondered what Jordan Baker, with her Southern roots, would make of what he said …

Marcus had joined the Navy at sixteen; he had been to Hawaii, the Philippine Islands, and Europe. He described the red-velvet chambers of Toulon bordellos, where a man could take his pick of whatever girls, boys and practices he fancied; he painted a picture of dockside dives in Manila that would fleece or even kill any sailor so unwary as to set foot in one alone. In the time of telling, his stories hauled our minds wholesale out of those long hot days by the Flushing River. Even as Marcus spoke of cruelty or perversion, the man's quiet tolerance, his stubborn and unreconstructed refusal to judge shipmates or overseers, seemed to acquire disproportionate presence, the way a statue spotlit from beneath threw a shadow much taller than itself. When Marcus's wife and daughter one day stepped off the Long Island local to have lunch with him we got a notion of the source and guarantor of those qualities.

Essie-Mae Fayerweather, a small and whip-lean woman, was even calmer than her husband, though she smiled more; though her eyes acquired edge and her mouth-line hardened when Myrtle, stopping by for coffee and to cadge money off Wilson, who had just lost big in a craps game in Greenpoint, made her habitual comment about the impropriety of "Negroes" sitting with white folks. All Essie-Mae did then was grip her husband's arm more tightly while Sarah, their ten-year-old, built houses of our spare set of cards.

"It's just words, Marcus," she whispered once Myrtle had left. And he nodded, glancing at Sarah, and murmured, "I know."

And George, looking uncomfortable; leaving to explain to his wife how, though he had no money for her today, he would surely have some tomorrow; touched Marcus lightly on the shoulder as he passed.

"She doesn't hate him," he told us later, while Marcus was walking Essie-Mae and Sarah back to the station. "Where Myrtle's from, in Jersey, well, they keep folks separate is all … She ain't happy here," he added unnecessarily. "When I was working for Lincoln, things was different. I made good money, we even had a car, a Lincoln of course, and a little house. I didn't, you know": he swept a large, greasy hand to indicate the game of stud Mike was setting up. "Not so much, anyway."

His big, guileless face had softened and his eyes looked elsewhere. It was rare for Wilson to open up like this; he spent most of the time complaining about his hand, frowning in concentration as he totted up the money he was losing.

Mike was often absent from our conversations. His poor English frustrated him—time and time again he would search for word or phrase and then, not finding it, would throw up his hands with an explosive "*Ga-MO-to!*"

Gamoto was uttered frequently that summer, and not just in conversation. Early each morning Mike would limp off to buy the papers at Flushing Station, looking for news of the Greek-Ottoman war, and the news was usually bad. The Turks were strengthening their army thanks to trainloads of guns and gold supplied by Bolshevik Russia. "*Rosia—Gamoto!*" Mike would yell, hurling the paper south; his pupils, under the shadow of those Olympian eyebrows, flared with rage. And every time I was reminded of my father, who taught his boys only one lesson in political economy but taught it often, with that Finnish blend of stolid calm and unquenchable determination: "Remember, never trust a Russian. Russia is the enemy, always and forever." He said this even after 1918 when the Bolsheviks, distracted by revolution, gave Finland her freedom. And I felt a stab of retrospective guilt when Mike brought up "*Rosia*" because it reminded me of my parents, whom I had left for the cash I could earn running hootch for a bunch of New York swells.

The stab was tiny, though—more of a pinprick. People from Finland, long used to murderous winters and the tender favors of the Okhrana, are good at stamping down emotion to begin with. I have already described how the steel and railroad trusts broke the Minnesota unions; how Seppo Kumpunen died in a fruitless brawl against their thugs and scabs; how losing people I loved changed the anger I once felt into a sour belief that the only path to survival was to look out for yourself. So I remained calm and detached, even after reading in Mike's newspapers about the railroad strike.

Almost half a million railroad workers had walked out that July. They had gone on strike to protest a cut in wages imposed by companies whose profits were actually increasing at the time. This, as it turned out, would be the Great Railroad Strike of 1922.

In response the companies hired scabs, and 16,000 thugs whom they deputized as marshals and sent to bust workers' heads in Cleveland, Buffalo, New Jersey. And while the old Jaan Laine would have supported the strikers' claims, the new "Jon"—former lieutenant (junior grade) in the US Navy, currently captain of a sleek and highly profitable rum-runner—figured they stood no chance of winning, and flipped to the sports pages. The bankroll in his pocket, fattened with a bonus and three weeks' pay, was evidence enough that he had chosen the right course.

But dead ideals leave unquiet ghosts. One afternoon, finishing a dish of meatloaf with mashed potatoes at Mike's, I watched as a family of dump-pickers: a father, mother and three children, dark-skinned in the manner of Mediterranean peoples or gypsies; walked down our road in the direction of the Land of Ashes. These pickers, I knew, made some kind of living by digging up whatever coins, earrings or other trinkets, lost in household rubbish, had found their way into ash-haulers' trucks and to the dump.

The pickers' clothes and faces were dusty, and all of them were thin. One of the kids had shoes too big for him, and as I watched he lost one shoe in the dust and had to turn to slip his bare foot back in. A younger child was riding a spavined trash-cart the father pushed. The woman walked slumped, as if beaten down by the weight of the smoked air above her. My meatloaf, which was unusually good, all at once turned as tasteless as the ash that family shuffled through.

I peeled a five-dollar note from my roll, walked out of the restaurant and handed the bill to the woman. She looked at it dully then, fast as a squirrel stealing a nut, stashed it in a pocket of her dress. The father thanked me and in an accent thicker than Mike's asked the way to the ash dump, which I pointed out—they should have turned north at the last block, I told them, as no pedestrian bridge existed here.

The giant pupils of Dr. T.J. Eckleburg looked over the pickers in disapproval as they turned and shuffled away. I went back to my meatloaf, which tasted savory again, and within a few minutes had forgotten that family completely.

Chapter Eight

The call for our second run came the day after I saw the dump-pickers. We only had twenty-four hours to prepare since for unknown reasons the agent in Canada had waited two days to notify Wolfshiem of the ship's departure. The second steamer, the *Loch Nevis*, had suffered engine problems which delayed its voyage; we would be meeting the *Loch Alsh* once more.

Despite the short notice, and thanks to Wilson's obsessive coddling of the Libertys, the run went smoothly enough, to begin with at least. I had to play around with the throttles, but by the time we threaded Throg's Neck I'd figured out the port engine pushed a little stronger than the others and had to be throttled back slightly at high speeds.

I even let Young Sam steer. He had, over the long, frustrating days of inactivity, lost most of his adolescent truculence, partly because he was at heart a friendly kid; mostly because he was curious about things and did not mind if those teaching him were, in his eyes, old men. He never talked much but paid attention to Marcus's stories and Mike's explanation of poker odds, and when something pleased him a grin would spread unfettered across his fat, pimpled cheeks and his eyes would squint in pleasure; as they did now while he steered northeast by north into Long Island Sound.

In the excitement of his new role as helmsman he forgot to be seasick. I pushed the engines to near full power and the *Daisy* lifted

herself half out of the water and took off headlong for Ireland. And
Young Sam whooped with joy.

No dark boat followed us from Little Bay or anywhere else. We
anchored in Stony Brook harbor as before and at 10:47 that night,
almost the agreed time, we saw the green lamp flash as *Loch Alsh*
hauled its dark shape across a patch of moonlight. Only a handful
of high clouds were present and the moon was three-quarters full,
which was not ideal for smuggling; and I made a mental note to ask
Gatsby to schedule runs, if possible, when the moon was new, or
less than a quarter full. Still, we had the assurance that Coast Guard
cutters would be somewhere else, we had our speed to fall back on
if they weren't.

The sea was a little calmer than it had been for our first rendezvous. The *Loch Alsh* took our lines; the loading gang scrambled
down the Jacob's ladder without fuss. One of them told me they
had an extra three dozen cases to transfer compared to last time—I
was pretty sure that was what he said, through a Scottish accent
strong enough to saw teak.

Once we got the rhythm established: drop the cargo net, unload
it on *Daisy*'s deck, fire-gang the whisky cases below and stack them
while the net was lifted back aboard the ship to fill again; it looked
as if we would be finished with time to spare to meet our unloading
deadline in Huntington Bay. I had gone below to make sure the
cases were braced tightly enough, and was putting my shoulder to
a pile of gin boxes to lean them against the boat's inner hull, when
through *Daisy*'s planks I heard a series of sharp pops that sounded
a lot like gunfire.

Someone shouted on the deck above. I ran topside. Young Sam
and three Scotsmen, who'd been pulling cases out of the net, were
looking aft, past the freighter's stern. No more "pops" came for a
minute.

"Och, that'll be the fookin' rozzers," one of the Scotsmen said
as a tiny flame sputtered in the dark east of us and seconds later a
ripple of machine-gun fire reached our ears again.

"Ros—what?" I asked the Scot.

"Rozzers—*po*-lice. Yer ain fookin' Coast Guard."

Marcus came up the hatch and I told him to get the engines running. "Cast us off," I yelled up to *Loch Alsh*'s deck, but nothing happened. "Hey," I yelled again, "we're casting off!" and someone shouted back, "The captain wants a word wi' ye."

I looked around. The Scotsmen were all watching me, Young Sam was watching me. I said to him, "Get ready to drop our lines."

"The captain," one of the Scotsmen objected, jerking his thumb upward. I wondered whether they would physically prevent us from untying.

Around us the waves and moonlight played shadow puppets with each other but no other shapes or boats were visible. Even in the direction from which the shots had come I now saw nothing.

Cursing quietly, I stepped onto the rope ladder and scrambled to the *Loch Alsh*'s cargo deck. A minute later I was standing on the port wing of the steamer's bridge. Heart pounding, I looked around the horizon and from this high a vantage point saw the distant steaming light of a large ship to the west; but that was all.

The *Loch Alsh*'s captain was a short man with a beard and peaked cap turned russet by the glow of the compass by which he stood. "Murray," he said, grasping my hand. "Ye've no need to cast off, this is British territory." His words rumbled through the "r"s like a stick against a picket fence.

"I'm not British," I said. "If that's a cutter and they come close, they can arrest my boat here, if they want to. Or they can wait for us to leave and then sink us."

"We've no got time," Murray said.

"Let go my lines."

"No."

We stared at each other. A sequence of flashes, farther to the southeast this time, was followed by another rip of automatic fire, then a few single pops. They petered out in the shush of wind.

"Cast us off," I said. "If it's not a cutter, it'll be hijackers—pirates. I'll take the boat close enough to see."

"Are you out of your mind?" Murray said, or I thought he said, since it came out more like "Air ye oot yair my-ind?", and I replied, "Once we're loose we can run circles 'round anything on this ocean."

Finally he agreed, albeit with bad grace. He would leave the green lantern shining so we could find him again. Back aboard *Daisy* I flicked the ignition switches and our Libertys rumbled to life. The Scotsmen climbed back up the Jacob's ladder, *Loch Alsh* dropped our lines, and I eased us away from the freighter's side. While Young Sam coiled rope, I opened the hidden locker and heaved out the Colt-Browning. I humped it to the cargo deck where I laid the machine-gun on whisky cases still littering the planks. Despite my fine words to Murray, I could not speed nor dodge too much with loose cargo aboard. Marcus came up from the engine room as I was checking the machine-gun's magazine.

"You know how to use that thing?" he asked.

"We had two on the subchaser."

"Huh." He stared at me. He knew I'd been an officer and thus unlikely to be assigned machine-gun duty. "You ever fire it?"

"There's a first time for everything."

Marcus shook his head. "God help us all," he said.

I goosed the throttles to one-third speed, leaned the *Daisy* in a gentle circle and headed southeast, in the direction from which we'd last heard gunfire. I got Young Sam and Marcus to stand on either side of the wheelhouse as lookouts. Although Wilson had finally fixed the underwater bypass, we only used it in harbor and we couldn't hear firing over the roar of our engines' exhaust.

After a couple of minutes two muzzle flashes happened slightly to port and I turned that way, slowly increasing to half speed. As the boat lifted, the cases on deck slid against the aft cabin but no further.

"What are you doing?" Marcus yelled through the wheelhouse door and I yelled back, "Just wanna make a pass, see who they are. Then we'll get the hell out."

We were moving at twenty knots by then, pounding on waves that were higher than they'd been earlier. The deep roll of "bangs" as *Daisy* hit each ridge of water filled my senses fast and hypnotic as the jazz drummer I'd heard so long ago in that club in Duluth. After two minutes Young Sam shouted, "There they are," pointing ahead and just to port.

I'd been holding course by compass and the binnacle light had drained my night vision, but when I looked in the direction Young Sam was pointing I could just make out two boats, only a few cable-lengths away, and mere yards from each other: a long, low launch with a square wheelhouse and a bigger boat, a schooner. Both were dark even where moonlight struck them.

At least they were not white. Coast Guard cutters had white hulls and they were not schooners, they were bigger than these boats in any case.

"Rum pirates!" Marcus yelled. I saw more flashes on the schooner, but if the fire was aimed at us we were too far away and going too fast to be hit.

I turned *Daisy* in a wide half-circle and headed on a reciprocal course, back the way we'd come. A hint of whisky, from unstacked bottles that had broken when I turned, rose like an errant dream from the companionway.

Wolfshiem was waiting for us at Huntington Bay; I saw the lava dot of his cigar as we maneuvered toward the dock.

So, to my surprise, was his niece. The hurricane lamps their unloading gang used to light a path to the motor-vans were few and kept dim to avoid unwelcome attention, but even in their daffodil gloom the smile Stella gave me lifted my spirits, which had been dragged down by the weight of worry over rum pirates, over the extra time it had taken to load because of them. The tint of approaching dawn was stronger than the last time we had docked here. I worried, too, about the wind, which was still strengthening, and backing now to the east.

"Heard there was a hijacking on the Sound," Wolfshiem growled. I was still looking at Stella; they'd both come aboard once the gang had got to work. Wolfshiem followed my gaze. "My usual driver wasn't around," he explained impatiently, "I don't—So did you see anything?"

I told him we'd seen plenty, though the hijackers tonight had hunted other prey. "A long dark motorboat?" he repeated. "Yes," I said, "maybe thirty, thirty-five feet. And a schooner, sixty, seventy feet, I'm not sure who was hijacking who, we got out of there fast."

Wolfshiem stared at the bay. The ash of his cigar glowed and faded, glowed and faded.

"Seen anything else, at the garage? Anything unusual recently? Or the restaurant," he added. "Short fat fellow in a long black coat—"

"With bedroom eyes," I finished for him. "Nope, nobody like that."

"Keep your eyes peeled," Wolfshiem said. "Not just for him. This bunch, the d'Aquilas, they figger they got rights … I'm workin' a deal with their rivals"—he stopped. "Well, that doesn't matter.

"But this guy, Mineo," he continued. "You remember that name: Mineo. You can do that, right?" He grabbed my upper arm with a strength that surprised me.

"You're doing a good job, Laine," he hissed, almost looking at me directly then, "but don't let your guard down now." And the genial expression he usually wore slipped for a second, and I saw the predator beneath.

I promised I would be watchful. Stella handed me a pay envelope as they left. "Goodbye, Mister Laine," she said, her teeth gleaming in a grin so strong that despite all the scares and rush of the night so far, it went down my eyes and chest to bounce around the tensioned grotto of my stomach.

They asked for Young Sam and took him with them, and a minute later were consumed by the fading but persistent dark.

When the latest bonus was included I had saved almost 2500 dollars in cash. For the first time I pushed for higher bet ceilings at our poker table, a request Wilson backed but which Mike rejected—in part, I think, out of concern for Wilson.

I walked to Flushing Main Street with greater regularity, and on one of those excursions bought the Victor Talking Machine Company phonograph I had looked at earlier, along with a dozen records. The recordings were all of ragtime, which was not my cup of tea but better than the symphonic or music-hall songs that were the only other choices available.

I brought back the phonograph, in its heavy mahogany cabinet, in a taxi, and Mike helped me carry it into the restaurant. I had decided against keeping it in my room. I spent the vast majority of my waking hours at Mike's anyway, and the thought of listening to music by myself was not as happy as it should have been. And it was fine to watch the faces of my comrades open like sunflowers as I wound the crank, gently lowered the needle; as the ripple of "Opera Rag," played on the pianoforte by Mr. Edward T. White, surged into a room that had never heard music other than the soft notes of poker calls and the tuneless whistle of our solitary cook-plus-waiter.

Myrtle was not there when I brought it in but Wilson ran to fetch her, and all of us watched in astonishment as she took George in her arms and, giddy as a June-bug, two-stepped him down the narrow alley between counter-stools and booths. Myrtle had hurt her nose a while back—she claimed she'd fallen against a couch at her sister's, though Mike figured Wilson had socked her, an idea which seemed to please him—and the bruise made her look unhappier than usual; but now her face was pinked from dancing and she gazed at Wilson with eyes narrowed in affection, and Wilson looked as pleased as if he'd won two hands of poker in a row.

If you excluded the phonograph music, poker, and the faces and tales of my companions, however, my memory of those days flowed into a film of drab colors: the stained walls and pine counter-top of Mike's, the dun of burning trash from the Land of Ashes. Sun snapping off the railroad's steel tracks, the bleached eyes of

T.J. Eckleburg above us all. In that continuum anything out of the ordinary stuck out like a Ziegfeld dancer at a Quaker meeting; such as the arrival of the phonograph, and the call I made to West Egg trying to raise Gatsby.

The telephone receiver was picked up on that occasion by a man with an accent like a Port Elizabeth stevedore trying to talk like King George V, who informed me that Mister Gatsby was not available, and would I like to leave a message.

When I asked, quite hopelessly, if Miss Baker happened to be present, he told me to wait—and when Jordan's voice against all odds came sparkling over the line I felt a ridiculous urge to weep. In my shock and delight I told her the truth. I wished simply to see her, in any shape or form, at any time she deemed acceptable and that Gatsby judged was compatible with my duties as the *Daisy's* captain.

And she said that would be nice. Though her aunt, with whom she lived, relied on her for errands, and she had to prepare for a golf tournament over the next week or so, she promised she would try to get away.

No runs were scheduled while Jordan practiced golf. Wilson passed on news that *Loch Alsh* was now anchored on Rum Row, off the southern shore of Long Island. The *Loch Nevis* was still laid up with engine woes, in Halifax now. No short fat man in a long black coat appeared on our street to observe us through bedroom eyes.

It was as if everyone was on holiday this month. The Turkish army had not moved, though an assault on Smyrna seemed imminent. The 400,000 railroad workers were still on strike but they were mostly maintenance men and yard workers; the unions representing engineers and machinists, whose wages had not been cut, did not join the action, and trains kept steaming and rattling over the drawbridge next-door. By now, the *Tribune* claimed, a total of ten railroad workers had been murdered by the forces of capital, and one guard had been killed in a fight.

And then, almost two weeks after my call to West Egg, the Great Railroad Strike came to us.

It arrived in the guise of our drawbridge, which around noon one day rose and was not lowered again; in the shape of a west-bound train, filled with city workers, that stopped at the raised bridge. Another train pulled up behind it, and another, all hissing in their frustration and immobility; the smoke and steam from their engines, billowing voluptuously, thickened the ash-fumes around.

A knot of six or seven workers clustered at the drawbridge, talking to the bridge attendant—strikers, I assumed, since the span still did not come down, though now and again a conductor or a few passengers would walk down the line and argue with the rail-road men, then leave, waving their arms in irritation.

Mike's had never seen such business. It was raining, for a change, in greasy showers that sprinkled, stopped, sprinkled again. Passengers left the stalled carriages, holding newspapers over their hats. They came looking for a telephone or taxi and stayed for Mike's coffee, eggs and ham. They mumbled, swore and paid a dime each to use George Wilson's 'phone. Taxis appeared then trundled off, weighted with more passengers than seemed safe, for New York.

Mike drafted me and Young Sam to help serve the sweating businessmen and flustered secretaries, the doormen and bus drivers, the clerks, cooks, and plumbers who on a normal day kept the city going. There was much cursing of unions, socialists and railroad workers. I was carrying three cups of coffee and two plates of ham, eggs and buttered toast when the restaurant went quiet.

People stared outside. Four cars that were not taxis had drawn up beside the train line. Fifteen or sixteen men piled out holding clubs and baseball bats. Three of them, in some kind of uniform, wore pistols on their belts. In a ragged group they marched toward the tracks, over the fence and up to the railroad men, who had gathered across the tracks to stop them.

It did not last long. The strikers were badly outnumbered. The two groups merged, clubs rose and fell. Two men tumbled off the bridge, still grappling. Finally three of the strikers were hauled off with hands tied behind their backs and after a few more minutes the drawbridge was lowered. In Mike's restaurant the passengers cheered, left coins on the table and sprinted for their trains.

Mike was in back, fetching another bag of coffee; we had run out of coffee in front. Young Sam was washing dishes. Stavros, taking advantage of Mike's distraction, was trying to interest one of the last train passengers in a game of "Follow the lady." I was clearing booth tables when one of the uniformed men came in, along with two fellows carrying lead pipes and another a bat. "A third one down at Fresh Pond junction," one was saying. "We got time," the uniformed man replied, and nodded at me. "We need coffee, and what else ya got?"

I stood there, holding a tray of dirty cups. The guard was broad, muscular, with thick lips and stoatish eyes of a blue so clear it seemed almost transparent.

I stood there, telling myself this was not my fight. This was no longer any business of mine. I had learned the hard way that you could not, must not, resist a force so much stronger than you; the only way to beat them, as the saying went, was to join them, even if they looked as arrogant and stupid as this guard in front of me.

Therefore I would now smile, suggest ham, eggs, and toast, and take their order.

Still I did not move. Kept standing there, smiling vaguely, as a small but solid cloud of what I later recognized as anger rose from deep within until it reached my voice.

And I said, "We don't serve scabs."

There was a beat of silence. Then: "*What* did you say?" the man with the baseball bat asked.

I cleared my throat nervously.

"We don't serve scabs here," I repeated, as politely as I could.

I didn't last any longer than the strikers had. All three of them came at me. I dropped my tray and stepped back, avoiding the bat's swings. The guard lunged past the batter, reaching for my throat and I managed to jab him in the face before the bat landed on my right arm with a jolt of pain so severe that some miracle of nervous energy caused lights to flash red in my left eye. In the corner of my other eye I caught a glimpse of Young Sam standing behind my assailants, still holding soiled dishes, his mouth open in panic. Give me a hand here, Young Sam, I thought. One of the scabs dragged me to the floor while the heavy guard kicked at my ribs and head. I tried to grab his foot and then both eyes saw stars.

Shortly thereafter the kicking stopped. I heard Mike's voice.

"You get out, *malaka*."

A pause.

"You don't wanna do that," the guard said.

"Get out, all you. *Now*."

The men who'd been holding me down rose slowly to their feet. I sat up, trying not to whimper. My right arm and ribs had holes in them and so did my face, at least that's what it felt like. I turned my head with difficulty in the direction Mike's voice had come from. He was standing at the storeroom door, a bag of coffee in one hand. In the other he held a twelve-gauge shotgun, aimed steadily at the guard's chest.

Chapter Nine

I didn't really expect Jordan Baker to make good on her promise. After the fight with the strikebreakers I felt lousy and looked worse. I had a black eye, a cut ear and cheek, and my arm, though it was not broken, was bruised enough that I couldn't move it without gasping. Overall I thought a two-bit brawler like myself could not go anywhere with a girl like Jordan and didn't deserve to either.

But as any gambler knows, it is sometimes when you're most certain you are going to lose that the sweet cards show, and on the third day after the fight I was washing my cuts in my room's tiny washstand when a knock came at the door and Wilson entered.

"You got a message," he said, and handed me a slip of paper. It read: "Mr. Bokannan, 5 PM, To Plaza Hotel. Miss Jordan Sed Gatsby Sed You Can Take Nite Off."

Wilson observed me with his usual expression, half dubious, half confused, as if he too wondered how he'd come to occupy this particular spot in space and time.

"You still look like shit," he remarked.

"Thanks," I said. "Who's Bokannan?"

"Fellow from East Egg. He's gonna sell me a car. Then he'll drive you to New York."

"Will she be there? Miss Baker?"

"Dunno," he added, and now he frowned slightly; of the many facets of existence that puzzled George Wilson the most mysterious,

I reckoned, would be anything to do with the other sex. In that, of course, he was not alone.

"Funny, I was wonderin'—" He kept watching me for a few seconds, then left.

"Mr. Bokannan" showed up a little after five in a shiny new Ford coupé of peacock blue. I didn't see him at first—I was in my room, peering at the clouded mirror over the washstand to make sure, despite the wounds and bruises, I'd look at least mildly presentable for the Plaza Hotel, which I knew was one of the swanker joints in the city.

It was hard to look in the mirror without seeing the daguerre-otype of Eiki tacked beside it. My ribs and arms still hurt but I figured that as long as I didn't have to fight anyone they'd be OK. I had taken a bath—no small feat, since I had to haul buckets of hot water from Mike's to Marcus's tin hip-bath to do so. My blue suit and new Panama still looked good, and I had polished my reserve shoes till they would have satisfied even Captain Nelson, who had commanded our fleet of subchasers and was a stickler for polish.

I was more than a little nervous. For one thing I was still unsure whether Jordan actually planned to meet me, or was just passing along Gatsby's offer of a night out. I decided to assume she'd be there. In this, perhaps, I was subconsciously influenced by the thought of how Jay would treat such worry—and I walked to Mike's for one of his special coffees, to take on some of the extra confidence whisky imparted, without spotting the car parked by the gasoline pump.

I'd had little to drink since Gatsby's party and the whisky-jolted coffee tasted fine. I was thinking of ordering another when I noticed movement outside, and a large man with a jutting chin, in a city suit; a man with straw-colored hair weeding out from under his straw boater, entered the garage forecourt. He was accompanied by George Wilson. They must have just come out of the garage, and they stood between pump and coffeeshop, talking. The blond man in the boater was even larger than Wilson, and he waved his arms to emphasize what he was saying.

"Mike," I said, "isn't that—the guy from the train, coupla weeks ago?"

"Yeah," he said, coming to the window near me, drying a plate on his apron and shaking his head. "That's the *malakas*. Iss how he met Myrtle, this four-flusher come to sell Wilson that nice Ford, but always he want too much money."

"And Myrtle—"

"Iss how they met," he repeated, and turned away, repeating "*malakas*."

"But," I stammered, "but, I mean Jordan—Miss Baker—told me to get a ride with him, but how come *she* knows him?"

"Because—" Mike's eyebrows drew down in a frown black as tornado weather. "This rich *malakas*, he is also friend to Miss Baker, an' Mister Gatsby too. The *malakas* want to *sell* his automobile, Miss Baker tell him Wilson garage want to *buy* automobiles." He waved a dishtowel to indicate the blindingly obvious nature of how people passed along to each other vital data on used motor vehicles.

I watched them for a minute or so. I didn't want to ride with a man who was walking out with Myrtle behind her husband's back. George Wilson was dull as a rock, except when it came to gasoline engines; he was a poor gambler and usually broke, despite the good money he made from the operation, and this was not the best way to please a woman like Myrtle; yet I did not doubt that he loved his wife, and deserved better than this.

But he was also what Jordan, or Gatsby, had arranged. And right now to leave this place where if you discounted minor incidents involving scabs, nothing ever happened; to put miles between me and the smoke-gagged wasteland we lived beside; to visit a city that of all the world's cities, it seemed to me, must hold the greatest concentration of spires and speed, of fair women and music—in this instant a ride to New York was all I wanted from life, and if Satan himself had showed up in that shiny blue Ford I think I would have accepted his offer of transport. So I left money for Mike and walked toward the garage forecourt, where Mr. Bokannan and George Wilson were still talking, eyeing the car beside the red pump.

—

"He won't take my price," Buchanan grumbled a few minutes later. (He had introduced himself, correcting Wilson's spelling in the process. We were bouncing down the ash track and into the first paved streets of Flushing.) "What the—"

A woman had stepped into the roadway to flag us down. Buchanan stopped the car. Myrtle Wilson stuck her head in my window and stared at me, her well-rouged mouth open in surprise.

"Mister Laine," she said. "What—?"

"What are you *doing*?" Buchanan said.

"I jiss needed a ride," Myrtle said.

Buchanan looked behind us. The garage, and Wilson, were out of sight behind the corner.

"Well, get in," Buchanan told her irritably. Seen from this close he had a cruel mouth, and an athlete's way of moving that was visible even while driving, as if he was used to marshalling all his muscles to act in one direction and with single intent. He would be a good man to have on your side in a fight, I thought, touching the cut on my cheek.

"Why didn't you take the train, as we said?" he asked Myrtle when we were moving again.

"I missed that train," she answered just as huffily.

"I know Mrs. Wilson of course, from the garage," Buchanan explained to me. I nodded noncommittally. We were turning onto the automobile bridge over the Flushing River; I could make out the "gio … & Sons" boathouse across the creek, and the smoke of burning trash rose more thickly than ever over the Land of Ashes, but it was blown behind our car by the southwesterly breeze and through all my discomfort—because of the situation; because of how Jordan, or Gatsby, had conned me into it—I was still conscious · of how the air now tasted clear as Gilbey's finest, and how the eyes of Dr. T.J. Eckleburg could not find me anymore.

And twenty minutes later we were speeding onto the Queensboro Bridge. The sight of it had the same effect on me as the first time I crossed it: those towers and massive cables pulling us onto the span over the city below to impart the illusion that everyone in our car had a role to play in such power and daring. It made me shove aside my qualms for a few seconds and glory in the prospect of spending time in such a place, with or without Jordan Baker.

The bridge seemed to affect Myrtle Wilson in similar fashion. She lunged forward from the back seat so that her right breast swung into my left arm and her face, flushed with heat and excitement, emerged between me and Buchanan. Her wide and flowered hat was jammed between our shoulders as she cried, "Oh Tom, I feel like I could fly, every time I cross this bridge!

"I belong here," she continued, "don't you think? Not in boring ole Willets Point." Buchanan said nothing.

She glanced at me as the car accelerated down the ramp. "My dad was skilled in business, you know, he had a plumbing supply service for all of North Jersey, we were going to move to Manhattan but my mother got sick—"

"Her mother worked in a watch factory in Bloomfield," Buchanan broke in, his lips curled in amusement. "Her job was painting the dials and hands with radium, always licking the paintbrush."

"Tom," Myrtle complained, "that's not—"

"It ate away her mouth, and then the rest of her face."

Myrtle sat back in her seat. Her voice came to us more softly. "My dad spent all our money on clinics," she said. A moment later she added, plaintively, "He *loved* her, Tom."

Buchanan sniffed. "We're just friends, of course," he told me in a voice so low it would be hard for Myrtle to hear over the rush of hot wind through our windows. "But it would be best if you didn't mention this to Wilson, eh?"

—

When I entered the Plaza Hotel, still unsure of who had summoned me there or why, I found Jordan Baker in the hotel's tea garden, waiting at a center table.

She was dressed in a white pleated frock with a low-hanging belt and a white silk jacket. The thin dolphin-scarf I'd first seen in Gatsby's car was wound around her neck, and a white hat in the usual cloche style covered her short, bleached-gold hair. I stopped in my tracks—I realized now that, lacking Gatsby's incorruptible optimism, I had never altogether vanquished the suspicion that I was responding to Gatsby's offer of a night off, and not to an invitation from Jordan. And I was still irritated at how she'd brought me here. But she looked as fresh and pretty as a bank of crocuses against the last of winter's snow, and as my worry and irritation melted I grinned in delight.

We ate triangular sandwiches of egg salad and smoked salmon: morsels so delicate they seemed to disappear down my gullet before my tongue had time to taste them properly; so small that having eaten half a plate I was still hungry, and ordered another. I preferred blinis but to the extent I tasted these delicacies found them pretty good.

We drank a perfumed tea called "Oolong." A place like the Plaza, Jordan said, could not afford to openly serve liquor, though you could order it for your room, sub rosa, if you were a guest. A string ensemble played Fox Trot tunes but no one danced and Jordan did not suggest dancing, for which I was thankful, given the state of my ribs. She asked me about the cuts on my face and I considered telling her a story that sounded less rough than the truth but finally said simply, "There was some trouble at Mike's."

And she laughed, high and loud, adopting her habitual stance, leaning back and examining me through those invisible bifocals.

We chatted, as apprentice New Yorkers do, of how we got here. Jordan knew about *Tuolomee* and how I'd met Gatsby through Tai's chandlery, but not much else. Keeping in mind his request for discretion I skipped the tugs, and the desperate depths I'd plumbed after the war and on St. Croix Avenue. I suppose I was trying to protect Gatsby from tarnish by association with such low-lifes as myself, but I was also seeking to make myself more acceptable to her. Jordan's image of Jon Laine, once I'd finished, must have resembled a St. Olaf student and naval officer whose family once ran a big firm that supplied ships throughout the Great Lakes.

Her own story was sunnier. She had left Kentucky, where her father did "something with money" and owned racehorses, to play in golf tournaments up north and to visit her childhood friend, Daisy, in East Egg. She met Jay at one of his parties and when he offered her a job—apparently Wolfshiem thought a society woman would be helpful to Gatsby in seducing investors—she accepted, taking advantage of an offer of residence from an aunt who lived on Long Island.

It was evening by then. We left the Plaza, crossed 59th Street, and entered Central Park. Rays of lemon-colored light from the setting sun, where they could squeeze between buildings, turned shadow darker by contrast among the copses and woodland walks; under graceful bridges of wrought iron spanning bridle paths. We walked side by side, quite close, and Jordan slipped her arm under my damaged arm, which hurt but I barely noticed. Her shoulder and sometimes thigh, where they touched mine, were warm and soft and as if by some process of kind contagion this touch made the response areas in my chest turn feathery and warm as well. Fireflies flashed code under plane trees, as they had on Gatsby's lawns.

"Ah love this place," she told me, squeezing my arm tighter, and I suppressed a gasp of pain. "It seems so, well—enchanted, don't you think?

"It's so different from home," she continued without waiting for a reply. "Everything just feels heavy in Louisville, even in winter when it's cool. Everything *smells* heavy, lahk bad perfume—jasmine and wintersweet, oh, and clematis. The aunts watch everyone from their balconies, and the Negroes are always in the shadows under the balconies, you know they're there to help of course but they weigh us down, oh lordy, they weigh us down."

We were strolling on a paved path that wound around a small, willow-skirted pond. In the distance a brass band played.

"You yankees don't know Negroes lahk we do," Jordan went on. Her voice was low, as if it came from a distance, from where she'd grown up. "They are more separate than here and yet closer to us at the same time." I thought of Marcus and his stories of the South, and what he would have thought of this line of talk; but to ask pointed questions is not the road to a pleasant evening with a woman to whom you are attracted, so in this area too I held my tongue—and in so doing endorsed, without thinking about it more, the frothy insouciance of those rich enough to ignore the blood, toil and muck amid which so much of the world lives; denying, at the same time, the principles I'd once espoused, since the Finnish Socialists' Federation accepted all workers as equals no matter their race or background, and condemned the separation of which Jordan spoke.

The park lamps had come on by then. It was almost full dark. A handful of stars pricked out of the indigo above. It was that moment of transition when night animals with different prey and ways of moving from day creatures come out of the places they hide in when sunshine strokes the world. At this hour all bets are off, and a breath of danger scares hackles up and down your neck. The path we followed forked between tall trees and a large outcrop of rock.

Uncertain of which way to go, we faced each other. Almost without thinking, though my heart began to pound with the risk, I put my arms around her. Instead of pulling away with one of her too-loud, back-bent laughs, as I'd expected, she folded toward me, and our mouths found each other.

Her lips were softer than those tiny sandwiches. Her breath tasted of tea and egg salad. When we stopped to fill our lungs she sighed, "Well," and I replied, "Well." The brass band played a distant polka. I pulled her close again, and now she did pull back and laugh and said, "Slow down, Jon, we have plenty of time," and I said "Do we?" and she said, "A cocktail?" and I answered "Yes, yes, oh yes."

—

We left the park and hailed a hack, telling the driver we needed refreshing at a place that served good drinks, at which he snorted,

"Ya gotta be more specific." "And music," I added recklessly, "jazz music, the best."

"Uptown," he grunted, and drove us north, much farther up Fifth Avenue than we'd gone with Gatsby. The streets here were less well lit, the passers-by mostly dark of skin. The driver stopped at 134th Street by a corner entrance. "Barron Wilkins Cabaret," he said, leaning around to look at us. "You're not dressed the way they like, but tell the doorman Leon sent you. Slip him a fin, he'll let you in." Clearly it wasn't the first time he'd used that line.

A tall black man in a top hat and tails opened the taxi door and handed Jordan out as I paid the fare and retrieved the scarf she'd left on the back seat. Seeing our clothes, the doorman barred the way to the entrance. I mentioned "Leon," which didn't impress him much, then offered my hand with a five-dollar bill in it. He looked at the money with cold contempt but stood aside, saying, in a curiously soft voice, "Welcome to tango night."

The club was in the basement: a wide room in red-and-gold-checkered motif filled with spinning fans, russet plants, gilded columns. A twelve-piece orchestra, playing brass instruments, and a gold-painted dance floor were surrounded by tables covered in crimson table-cloths. The tables, sagging under ice-buckets crammed with champagne bottles, were encircled in turn by pale people in evening dress.

A pretty, caramel-skinned woman in a long rose gown showed us to a table where Jordan ordered something called "Fallen Angel": while I, harking back to the artillery-strength French 75s at Gatsby's, ordered a simple Scotch-and-soda highball. We sat close, not touching, watching a handful of couples attempt South American moves with North American feet. The music was loud and, to my mind, repetitive and stilted; very different from what I remembered of that Chicago band in Duluth, and not what I'd expected from New York.

The whisky was good, though, and I wondered if Barron's was one of our clients. We ordered a second round. I asked a waiter if another band would be playing different music, and he shook his head as if I'd asked a really stupid question and simply said, "It's *tango* night." I touched Jordan's arm and kept my hand there; she moved neither away nor toward me and I thought, or rather felt, that in a club like this full of people in white tie and two-hundred dollar gowns: a club tight with tunes that slinked and tripped along, regular as a clock; what chance Jordan and I had of touching each other more closely, mentally or physically, would suffocate and die.

"Let's go," I said, and she looked at me in relief.

The air outside, though still hot, seemed cool after the club. We walked a couple of blocks without direction. I was trying to remember the name of the jazz joint Stella Wolfshiem had suggested. The thought of her dusky eyes made me feel unaccountably sad. A taxi slowed upon spotting us and I asked the driver, who was black and presumably local, if he knew of a place called "Edmond's Cellar." He examined us with a slight, pitying smile and said, "Get in."

—

An hour later I was dancing with Jordan. The eyes of Stella were long forgotten and my bruised ribs and arm were giving me no trouble at all.

Edmond's Cellar was, as the name implied, underground, but that was all it had in common with Barron's Cabaret. It had no dress code or top-hatted bouncer and, to begin with, no music; the band was taking a break. The place was filled, wall to wall, with cigarette smoke and chatter from a mostly black crowd, but including a couple dozen white people, dressed in every style possible. No tables were free so we shared one with two mixed-race men who greeted us affably, their arms laced around each other in an attitude so intimate that I was, at first, nonplussed. Jordan, upon noting it, looked at me with wide eyes, leaning further back than I'd ever seen her lean. Then she opened her eyes wider yet, and grinned.

Fallen Angels were not on the menu, a waiter told us; we switched to something called "The Bee's Knees," a large glass filled to the three-quarter mark with the kind of gin that had never seen the inside of *Daisy's* hull, topped with a syrup so sweet it seemed to suck the enamel off my teeth. We drank two each before a band climbed onto the tiny stage up front.

People clapped and stamped their feet and yelled encouragement. The chatter died down; a portly man at the piano pulled a skitter of notes up and down the keyboard, then slowed to a rollicking, rhythmic tune on the lower keys. A couple of horns fell in with the beat, and increased in volume; then a very tall, beautiful woman walked to center-stage. She had close-cropped hair, a slightly hooked nose, and a swan's neck, and long tan fingers which she wove in and out of a strengthening skein of music. Her hips wove in and out of the curves her fingers drew. The woman's voice was soft in texture and acrobatic in range but what drew me in, what got my heart beating almost as fast as when I kissed Jordan, was how the song itself, entrained by the rolling melodic lines of trumpets and piano, pulled time back on itself, then released it, pulled and released, in a way that evoked exactly what you felt when you kissed a woman—when time stopped, flooded long, stopped again, then flooded more. It spun whole landscapes of harmonics between the lyrics, then meshed with the words she sang:

> *I never*
> *felt*
> *So lonesome before ...*
> *My man has*
> *quit me*
> *This time he's gone*
> *for sure ...*
> *And he broke my*
> *heart,*
> *Now I'd like to break*
> *his face ...*
> *For lettin' another*
> *woman ...*
> *Ease into my place*

Half the people were dancing now. Jordan still leaned in that extreme way, observing everything from hold-back: I couldn't tell if she felt anything from the music, let alone what I felt. The band started on a song that had the same strong pull and charge as its predecessor but was faster, more upbeat. Drawing on the space that kissing had filled in Central Park, I held out my hand, half-expecting her to demur, but she took it without hesitation and we wove our way to the floor.

There, holding each other, we moved—I cannot put it better than that—moved in a box step that was the only step I knew, but jacked and loosened by this tune that was so much more than a waltz. In the same way that the jazz dragged time back and apart, then reassembled it in a different rhythm, it seemed to pull the joints out of our hips and knees and spine to reconnect them along the lines it played.

I was a poor dancer but between the music and the gin my body felt as if it knew where to go and she followed willingly. We drew ever closer as we danced, our bodies touching everywhere they could, and for a moment I felt happier, more alive than I could remember ever having been since Eiki.

We danced to a slower song, then a faster. People shouted approval of the band; a man yelled at the singer, "Shake your *ass*, Mama String Bean!" and she winked at him, and did as he requested. Once we got in the way of a woman who was even taller than the singer, who told me to watch my step in a voice so deep it made me stare at her in surprise. Only then did I notice the shadow of a beard, the breadth of her shoulders, the lipstick adorning the features of the man she danced with. And by then the singer had been joined by another woman who clung to her like ivy on oak as they moved together to the song the first woman sang.

I had seen women who openly loved women, and men who loved men, in a sailor's bar in Corfu Old Port. Looking around me now I figured a quarter of the dancers were paired with someone of the same sex and though surprised, because I had never seen this in Minnesota, I was not particularly shocked. But I felt Jordan's head turning this way and that as she watched. Her cheeks gleamed with sweat, and her grip on me grew tighter. The heat we were making where we touched was high and seemed to call for kissing. When I came up for air and looked at the band again, I found the tall singer watching us. And she smiled, before turning back to her partner.

We grew thirsty and sat down again to drink. Jordan and I had both drunk a lot already but I did not feel drunk, only filled with a reckless energy. The band stopped then—"Straight from her recording session with Black Swan Records, Miss Ethel *Waters!*" a manager shouted. A tidal wave of applause and whoops rolled through the club. "Ricky Biggs on horn. An' Mister Fats Waller on keyboard!"

Jordan left to find a powder room. I observed the people around me with great benevolence, and sipped my gin rickey—I had quit ordering Bee's Knees, the taste of which, like the French 75s at Gatsby's, proved too sugary for my palate. My earlier joy had turned more mellow but of an equally pleasant wavelength in which everyone I saw seemed lovely and every embrace, regardless of propriety, a direct consequence of such beauty.

I was so content and pleased with everything that when a shift in crowd dynamics opened a line of sight toward the powder room, and I saw the tall singer talking to Jordan—smiling at her with head cocked, then draping both arms over Jordan's shoulders and slowly, languorously, kissing her, a kiss from which Jordan did not lean away—my first thought was only how right it seemed that the two woman for whom I felt the most in this amazing club should be as attracted to each other as I was to them.

She must have seen me watching for Jordan sat down without looking at me. Her cheeks were pink but so were mine probably. The temperature in Edmond's, both internal and external, seemed to have tripled over the last half hour. The band started up again and the tall woman, Ethel, began to sing. I held out my hand once more, Jordan took it as readily as before, and we moved back onto the floor.

My train is
leavin'
I got the down-home
Blues
Woke up this morning,
The day was
Dawning,
And I was feeling all sad and …
Blue …

———

There are times in a man's life when the solid steel rails on which you have run so far cannot accommodate the speed you have for one reason or another attained; then, jumping the rails, you enter a terrain you could never have anticipated and will never visit again.

My night with Jordan Baker was one of those times. When we left Edmond's Cellar I recognized neither the street, nor anything else that had been familiar to me, except for her. The idea of separating seemed at once dangerous and wrong, and she must have felt the same because when we finally found a taxi she told the driver, without looking at me, "The Metropole Hotel."

In the room we rented, Jordan and I made love to each other as if our survival depended on it; as if, should each body not become part of the other, the everyday world—built as it was to keep us apart—would crush us the second we said goodbye.

We lay for hours in a stilled hurricane of sheets. Through our window, which unlike my previous room's faced west, we watched the lights of New Jersey tremble over the swart aortal flow of the Hudson River. The thought that we might never again lie in the same bed was really a feeling: it was neither backed up nor contradicted by facts, but allowed to exist in that place out of space and that time beyond clocks which the music at Edmond's had opened for us, and into which we had once again plunged in the process of loving.

Yet I felt that in such a place impossible questions could be both posed and answered, so I went to the heart of my thoughts and feelings and said, "Do you think we will do this again?"

"I don't know," Jordan said, after a beat or two. "Probably not."

I half-agreed with her but that did not stop my gut from clenching, albeit mildly, with melancholy. I had been too happy too recently to accept without protest the return, however likely, of a common solitude.

"Why not?"

She stirred beside me. We'd been lying on our backs, my good arm pillowing her head. Now she raised herself on one elbow and held the sheet to her breasts as she looked down at me. Her milky-gold hair fell forward, framing her small, arrogant face.

"You know why not."

"Because I'm not one of your set."

"That's not it."

"Why, then?"

She sighed, dropped the sheet, and slowly lay down again: she had the same easy control of her muscles Buchanan had—that Jay Gatsby, I now recalled, possessed as well. Was everyone in their crowd a sportsman? I wondered vaguely. She put one hand, palm down, on my chest and moved it, also slowly, in a circle.

"Ah loved tonight, Jon," she said. "Ah love how carefree you are, and that allowed—oh, I don't know. I need a cigarette."

She got out of bed to find her purse. In the haze of lights the city projected on our window her naked body was a pale parenthesis, a curve that both framed and withheld. The match, in flaring, emphasized her cheekbones, the set of her jaw, the jut of her small breasts and nipples; I got a glimpse of how she might look on the golf course, her entire being bent on swinging a nine-iron in the most precise arc possible.

"I never really think of myself as carefree," I told her, after she had lain down beside me again.

"Well, you're not exactly care-full, are you? You're a rum-runner.... But the thing is, Jon, I need that. I need someone careful. Someone honest."

I was stung.

"You're not exactly 'careful' yourself," I said. "Look at the stunt you pulled to get me here tonight."

She blew a long plume of smoke toward the window. The smoke was blue against the glow.

"What does that mean?"

"Getting that fellow Buchanan to pick me up at the garage, when he's having an affair with George Wilson's wife? Don't tell me you didn't know."

"It seemed convenient," she said, after a pause. I could not see Jordan's eyes but I felt her looking at me. "You're shocked." Now she sounded amused. "You're not angry with me?"

"I just don't think it's fair," I said, "that's all." I sat up and put my left arm around my knees. For the first time since Central Park I was conscious of my aching ribs and arm. "Wilson—he's not a bad person, he doesn't deserve—"

"Oh Lordy," Jordan interrupted. "Nobody *deserves* anything." She reached out with one hand, and playfully flicked my forelock away from my eyes. "You think Daisy *deserves* it?"

I said nothing for a few seconds. Just like the last time she had uttered that name for those first few seconds I thought, stupidly, she was talking about our boat. I felt a tiny rush of affection for the *Daisy,* and I thought Jordan was right: something so graceful, so innocent of the plots and trickeries of her people, deserved better than what we were putting her through. Then it clicked.

"You mean Gatsby?" I said. "You mean, his girlfriend—the one named—"

"Light dawns on Marblehead—as you yankees say."

"Daisy—she's *married?*"

"To Tom Buchanan. Your chauffeur. You didn't know?"

"No."

"I thought everyone knew. Heck, Daisy knows *all* about Tom's girlfriend. Ah don't see what the big deal is ..."

I lay back on the bed. The sheets were damp and smelled of my sweat, and hers. I wanted a drink and a cigarette, and knew at the same time that all the gin and tobacco in the world would not make my world any less confusing than it was right now.

I felt, all of a sudden, a long, long way from Minnesota.

The Bee's Knees

ingredients

2 ounces gin
1 ounce strained fresh lemon juice
3/4 ounce honey syrup*

instructions

Combine all ingredients in a mixing tin. Add ice
and shake well. Strain into a chilled cocktail coupe.
Garnish with a twist of lemon peel

* Honey syrup: combine one part honey
to one part hot water

Chapter Ten

I got back to Flushing mid-morning. My head, oddly enough, felt clear of liquor. But I was tired from the nearly sleepless night, and still confused by everything to do with Jordan Baker.

I had thought about her endlessly on the assorted trains to Queens, but still was not quite sure what she meant by my being "careless," or dishonest. Of course I was engaged in illegal activities but so was she, and up to her fine Kentucky neck at that. Bootlegging and rum-running were felonies but they were crimes half the country condoned. Did she really want a straight arrow who would never contemplate breaking the antic law, or telling a lie? Did such a person even exist? And could someone like Jordan, who I was fairly sure got a kick out of twisting if not breaking every rule in the book, spend a day, let alone her entire life, with someone as lily-pure as that?

Speaking of rules, I knew that I had broken one by not getting back to the garage last night: Gatsby had given me the "night" off, according to Jordan, but not a blanket furlough. Yet there was no indication of the freighter being anywhere close, and even if news had come while I was gone, enough extra time was built in for us to meet it with hours to spare. So I figured that Wilson, who was in charge of the duty roster, might ride me a little about going AWOL, but no more. I was not prepared for him charging out of the garage as soon as I showed up that morning and aiming a pistol at my chest.

His washed-out features were wrung in rage; his eyes had narrowed and freckles burned like hazardous-cargo lights across his cheeks. "Where the hell have you been?" he half-yelled, half-hissed, striding up to me where I had paused to unlock the side-door to our warehouse on the way to my room. He stopped only a couple of feet away with the gun almost poking my navel. "Where did you *take* her?"

"George," I said, raising both hands palms out in what I hoped was an easily understood signal of "Don't shoot." "What's going on? What's—"

"I asked *you* a question."

"Okay." My pulse hammered at my ears. I tried to control my breathing, to radiate an image of inoffensive calm—of being "careful," as Jordan might have counseled. "I was in the city—"

"I *know* you were in the city. Where did you *take* her?"

The idea of George Wilson being concerned about where I went with Jordan Baker seemed out of all proportion to the gun in his hand, the muzzle of which wavered as his hand trembled. I saw myself then with a hole in my belly, life gushing away on the doorstep of a dusty rum depot in Queens while the eyes of Dr. Eckleburg watched me, uncaring, over Wilson's shoulder.

"I went—George, now wait, listen. Why don't you put the gun away?"

"I asked you a *question!*" he howled. The gun barrel wavered further. It was an Army Colt, a .45 caliber. Despite the waver it would not spare my gut.

"We went to the Plaza, but—"

"I *know* you went to the Plaza, you *bas*-tard! I mean afterwards or—or, you actually *stayed* at the Plaza *Hotel?*"

Young Sam came out of Mike's now, his mouth gaping in fear. Help was not going to come from that quarter. But something in the coupling of anger and astonishment in Wilson's words gave my tired brain, for the first time, a clue to what was going on in his.

"George—wait. Just tell me this: who do you think I was with at the Plaza?"

"My *wife*, you goddam son of a bitch! Don't smile like that, or I swear—"

Young Sam was ten feet away now, pimples near popping from stress, and I realized with astonishment that he was thinking of intervening. I flapped one hand in his direction, to stop him.

"I'm not smiling, George," I said hastily, turning my mouth down. "Only, you got it wrong. I wasn't with your wife—I wasn't with Myrtle."

"*Liar.*"

"Mister Wilson," Young Sam said in a voice high with strain, "please—"

"Sam," I began.

"Don't," Young Sam added.

"Shut up!" Wilson yelled at him, then turned back to me. "She was gone all night, and so were you."

"But I wasn't with Myrtle. I was with *Jordan*. Jordan Baker."

I watched his face not change, at first; then it did alter, the anger channels breaking, his eyes climbing out of their sinkholes of desperation.

"You're lying," he said, but with less conviction now.

"She gave you the message, by phone! It was to meet *her*, Jordan—not Gatsby or anyone else. You can call her to check. Or call Gatsby.... I wouldn't take Myrtle anywhere, George," I continued in what I hoped was a trustworthy, soothing tone. "You can put away the gun," I added; but he kept it aimed at my stomach, as if reluctant to lose the one lever he possessed to pry out truth from wherever it might be lurking.

He believed me, eventually, or at least accepted what I'd said for the time being—shook his head, though his eyes were still narrowed in suspicion as he let the pistol drop to his side.

And slumped away, back to the garage.

"I was worried," Young Sam told me excitedly, "when I saw that gun." I figured he'd been trying to compensate for his inactivity while I was being beaten by the railroad guards, and bought him a coffee and slice of pie in gratitude.

Then I climbed upstairs to my room, nerves still buzzing in the aftermath of risk. I lay on my bed, hoping to catch up on sleep.

But the nerves, and the recurring questions about Jordan, would not let me rest. Eiki's eyes in the daguerreotype watched me reproachfully within my room, and the eyes of Dr. Eckleburg watched me grimly from without. Three quarters of an hour later I heard George downstairs, yelling high again, then Myrtle's voice as she yelled back in lower, more dangerous tones. I jumped up, ran to the window. If Wilson was ready to confront Myrtle's supposed lover with a pistol, it followed that he might do violence to his wife. I wasn't sure what I could do against a gun, but felt I must do something.

They were inside the garage by then, their voices rising and falling, loudly at first. But after five or six minutes, intervals of softer, more conciliatory talk occurred, and I figured the danger was past.

—

By noon I still had not slept. I was at Mike's, chasing down the ham and eggs special with Mike's welterweight coffee, when Wilson came in. He looked around the room.

No one was playing poker. Mike was at the grill, Marcus was on the *Daisy*, Young Sam was eating scrambled eggs and reading the funny papers at the counter. One of Wolfshiem's part-time guards read a different paper and a couple, either from Flushing or badly lost, drank coffee at a far booth. Stavros was eyeing them with professional interest, and Mike was eyeing Stavros suspiciously while frying onions. Wilson lumbered to my table. I noticed he was not carrying a gun. His hands were even empty of the oil rag he usually carried. He sat down opposite me.

"I came to say sorry." His face was more emptily handsome than usual, a space of melancholy and persistent wonder at the world's complexities. His hair was mussed, his eyes gone back to their usual blurred azure. He laid his hands on the table and looked at them as if unsure of just what they were up to. "I should never have pulled a gun on you."

"Myrtle straighten you out?" I asked, and he nodded.

"She was at Catherine's. Her sister's, uptown, for the night—she just forgot, she didn't tell me."

He looked out the window. I followed his gaze. Where Myrtle's cheating was concerned I had been an innocent bystander, but I felt guilt nonetheless since I had, in some small way, gone along with her escapade.

"Well that's settled," I said cheerfully, expecting Wilson to leave; but he stayed where he was, staring at his hands again.

"People don't understand," he burst out, "she's flighty … seems so sure of herself but she's not, she's like a little girl sometimes."

Now one of his hands dipped below the table and I flinched, but he was only going for his rag, with which he slowly, carefully, wiped the palm that did not grip the cloth.

"She wants the good things," he said, watching his rag, "like nice clothes and stuff, who can blame her? But half the time she don't know what she wants, and even then she changes her mind the next day, know what I mean?" He looked up at me almost pleadingly.

"I could give her that," he continued, without waiting for an answer. "I gave her a real good life, in Detroit. If we'd-a stayed on, I coulda got another job, but she wanted New York City, it was what she always dreamed of."

"Maybe," I suggested carefully, "if you laid off the cards for awhile, you could … Wolfshiem must be paying you—" He shook his head, and switched rag hands, wiping his other palm as carefully as he had the first.

"I got in the hole with a big game in Astoria. I still owe them. If I could just win big, just one time—"

It was the usual gambler's excuse and I nodded, remembering Jordan's reply when I mentioned Wilson to her: "Nobody *deserves* anything."

Perhaps, I thought, she had a point. Maybe in this world what was truly right or wrong was so hard to nail down that feeling sorry for the victims was a waste of time. In such a world it was best simply to ditch regret and go for what was most expedient. "When thou hast been compelled by circumstances to be disturbed in a manner, quickly return to thyself and do not continue out of tune longer than the compulsion lasts," Marcus Aurelius advised. It was the path I had chosen, after all, following Seppo's death, and Eiki's.

Wilson got to his feet then. He nodded at me coolly as if, now he had apologized, we were back on an equal footing. The deferent tone he'd once used with the *Daisy*'s skipper, I noted, was quite gone; had been gone for a long time, I realized now. He spotted the funny papers Young Sam was reading, snatched them from the boy's hands, and left.

I watched him go, feeling as if his melancholy had rubbed off on me somehow. He was a man, I reflected further, to whom things happened, not the other way around. I needed to remember that so as not to fall into the same trap. And I turned my attention back to lunch.

—

Despite my high intentions about making things happen and not vice versa, I spent the next few weeks moving back and forth at the behest of Wolfshiem and Gatsby, in thrall to vagaries of sea, machinery and the trade in hootch.

Wolfshiem in particular had been spooked by the hijacking we'd witnessed on our last run, which word on the street claimed had been set up by one of the Italian gangs he was worried about. He told me over the phone it would be safer for the *Daisy* to leave Queens for a while, and this was an idea I did not disagree with. On top of that, with the *Loch Nevis* still laid up, *Daisy* and her crew needed to earn our keep; and I was ordered to bring our boat around Long Island to the south shore, to back up Wolfshiem's, as opposed to Gatsby's, segment of the operation—the low-rent, high-volume one.

We left before dawn on a blustery day at the tail end of July. It was a long haul and we had to refuel halfway, at Long Island's eastern tip, at the Montauk docks. Once we left Montauk and rounded Shagwong Reef and Phelp's Ledge we were in real ocean.

A ten-knot wind from the south kicked up wide swells three or four feet in height. The *Daisy*, with her flat, shallow bottom, was not a good boat for open sea and we had to reduce speed for the run westward, down Long Island's southern strand. She rolled and pitched with such enthusiasm that Young Sam got seasick again and spent that part of the trip leaning over the side, making unpleasant noises.

The ocean flank of the island was not a pleasant place for boats in general. Almost all of it consisted of a barrier beach with very few breaks and even these were defended by a frieze of offshore sandbars. As we progressed westward at a quarter speed we ran a form of highway between a fleet of schooners, big yachts and small freighters—including, somewhere, the *Loch Alsh*—anchored just over three miles from land.

Rum Row. Occasionally a small boat would dart from a break in the surf to a rum ship. And once, a sleek, white-hulled Coast Guard cutter appeared to the south, but it never came near the *Daisy*.

We'd been told to meet a local fisherman named Al Tibbets at a gas buoy off the Fire Island Inlet, 70-odd miles west of Long Island's tip, but though we waited by the buoy for over an hour he never showed.

It was near sunset by then. The swells were breaking, vicious and bone-white, against sandbars protecting the inlet. No channel or inshore buoys were visible—I learned later that local rum-runners had removed buoys to confound pursuers—and I had no intention of trying to find my way across the bar unaided in the growing dusk.

Finally I ran down a small boat coming in from Rum Row and offered its skipper money if he would guide us through the shallows. We settled on fifty dollars as piloting fee, but the fellow seemed reluctant; and I found myself worrying, as we approached the crash and welter of surf, that the man would lead us into shallows that his little dory would pass over but we could not, leaving a drowned crew and a broken boat whose remains he would strip at leisure, since wrecking was a traditional activity on any such coast.

I ordered Marcus and Young Sam to break out life jackets as the water between the foaming breakers turned light jade, then yellow: as claws of surf swiped at *Daisy*'s side and streaked the wheelhouse windows; expecting every second the fatal hesitation as our keel hit sand, and then the crash as the Atlantic hammered *Daisy* down against the deadly bar.

But soon the water deepened to dark green again and half an hour later, as Marcus and I were trying to figure out on the chart which of the many creeks and coves concealed Al Tibbets' dock, a boat rowed by a small, deeply tanned man appeared off our starboard side to guide us in.

—

We stayed at Tibbets' Cove for close to a month. In retrospect, of all the months I spent in Gatsby's employ, this turned out to be the most pleasant, to begin with anyway. We made six runs to the *Loch Alsh*, which were difficult technically because we could only go out when the tide was high enough and the sea calm enough to cross the bar; and because the swells offshore forced us to use myriad bumpers and two men to fend us off the freighter as we pitched in tandem to the Atlantic's beat. Even so there was always damage to repair.

Also, Wolfshiem's agent at Coast Guard headquarters did not have access to South Shore schedules, and the cutters were active here. Twice we had to escape them by speeding down the coast, once with a full cargo. But even loaded and in ocean swells *Daisy* ran twice the speed of the Revenue craft, and we circled safely back to Tibbets' Cove.

The cove itself was everything our home port was not. We lived where we unloaded at Tibbets' clam shack, a creaky structure of driftwood planks built on pilings over marsh grass and salt water. We moored the *Daisy* at an adjoining, even flimsier, dock, or anchored in the cove when the other launch was in. No houses were visible from here, making it an ideal unloading spot. The air smelled sweet from the surrounding white-pines and cattails, except at low tide when the odor of weed and muck took over, but even then it felt pure and healthy compared to the smoke and filth of the Land of Ashes. After a week my cough had all but disappeared. For the first time, by swimming in the cove and rinsing off with water from a rain barrel, I could bathe as often as I liked.

Most of the *Daisy*'s crew were content to be here also. Young Sam, who I suspected had not, till now, left the city for more than a day, was nervous at first, especially at night; everything was so silent around us, except for the wind and the occasional cry of loon, gull or owl, that he instinctively felt, as he would in Brooklyn, that bad things must be happening since the neighborhood was holding its breath. But after a few days and nights when, apart from trucks collecting liquor from where we stored it in a nearby barn, no strangers showed, he relaxed. And soon he was happy, when off-duty, to do nothing but laze in the sun and wade after blue crabs in the creek....

Wilson drove out after every run to service the engines and sometimes stayed the night in one of the shack's wooden bunks. By now he had fully accepted Myrtle's lies and forgotten his suspicions of me, and we talked normally about exhaust bypass and fuel systems. When he stayed overnight he lost some of his sempiternal pallor and the melancholy that rode with it—and then he talked of subjects that did not have to do with *Daisy*, or Myrtle's complaints, or his gambling debts: about a small garden that, as a kid, he tended with his mother, and the vegetable stand at which they sold produce. Or about his house in Detroit, that was big enough for a family, which he had hoped for but that Myrtle—and then the conversation did shift back to his wife.

Sometimes, more rarely, he talked baseball. He seemed to love the Brooklyn Dodgers almost as much as he loved engines. The only time I ever heard him speak ill of our employers was when he told me Wolfshiem's outfit had helped fix the 1919 World Series: this he didn't think was right. I asked him, if this were true and everybody knew about it, how come Wolfshiem and Gatsby weren't in jail. Wilson didn't have an answer to that and I figured it was just another tale invented by people who didn't know Gatsby, to explain his riches, and dismissed it out of hand.

Toward the end of our stay Wilson uncovered Al Tibbets' cache of handlines and hooks and after work would spend hours sitting on the wharf, once in a while catching scup or eel or sea robin but mostly, as far as I could make out, reveling in the kind of release from time, noise and expectations that fishing confers on its adepts. In those hours, I believe, he was the most peaceful I'd ever known him to be.

Marcus was the only one who did not care for our new billet. He hated the mosquitoes that came out at sunset and which, it was true, were a curse. He spent as much of his time as possible at a roadhouse called, unoriginally, the Dew Drop Inn. This was a dank, badly lit place of beer-pickled stucco, leaky shingles and low expectations, situated a ten-minute walk from our clam shack through pine woods and a potato farm. It stood on South Country Road, the principal thoroughfare linking South Shore towns.

The owner of the Dew Drop, a snake-eyed fellow named Conklin, did not want to serve Marcus, but with encouragement from Al Tibbets (who had married Conklin's cousin) and a generous per diem in both cash and hootch, he consented to let our crew use the bar's back-room where, conveniently enough, the telephone was also kept. Except for breakfast—campfire coffee and stale bread—we ate all our meals at the Dew Drop. The telephone there was our only link to Gatsby and Wolfshiem, and Marcus and I split the task of coordinating by 'phone with the trucks when we were set to make a run.

I used the Dew Drop's telephone to keep in touch with Jordan. Or rather, I tried to keep in touch with her that way. I had forgotten, during our night together, to ask if she had a telephone at her aunt's, and so could only leave messages with Gatsby's butler, or at Wolfshiem's office; but Stella, whenever I left a message at Mandala Holdings, responded with such sarcasm—"Still tryin' to romance your lady love, Mister Laine?" was one such response—that, suspecting she would not bother passing-on the messages, I stopped leaving them with her.

I got one message back from Jordan, via butler and Dew Drop. It came almost three weeks after she and I spent that night together, and after I had left at least a dozen messages at Gatsby's. It said only that she was very busy but would get in touch when she could. While I was unskilled in the codes pretty women employed to communicate with suitors, I was fairly sure that, once decoded, it would read "I have lost interest in you."

"Carefree …" That word floated like a refrain in my mind. I was still half in love with Jordan, despite what she thought of me. I'd been half in love with her even before we met at the Plaza, and the welding together of contrasts I'd experienced that night—holdback and headlong in her gaze and way of moving, softness and steel in her aspect and touch—had melted my feelings into an emotional alloy that I thought much stronger.

When I had work to do, on the runs or repairing the boat's bulwarks, I was happy enough. But when the work was done, and especially at night, I found myself obsessing over the feel of Jordan in memory: the touch of her lips on mine, the caress of her hands on my neck and back, the clear note of her voice in passion. I heard her high laugh in the call of loons, and in the marsh grass smelled the sugar of her sweat.

Mostly, and far too often, I went over what she'd implied about my carelessness, my dishonesty. Though it filled me with despair, because doing so processed an equation of heart she no doubt already had worked through, I worried at the factors of indifference and loss till finally I reached a result: that Jordan considered herself, also, to be careless and dishonest, and wanted the company of someone as different as possible so that union with him (or her; I had not forgotten the languor of the kiss she'd shared with the singer at Edmond's) would unite the varied facets of their personalities to make a whole. But I was not as carefree or dishonest as she assumed—or so I longed, desperately, to argue, would she but give me the chance.

—

I grew used to the lack of contact with Gatsby; accustomed to the likelihood that our friendship—never very deep, despite what appeared to be real pleasure on his part when we'd met again, and when he'd seen me at the party—had shallowed further over the time I'd worked for him. I'd not had news of him, if you excepted the rare occasions when the butler called on his behalf to check on runs with Marcus.

Yet on a morning of clear weather toward the end of our stay in Tibbets' Cove I received a message from Gatsby that had nothing to do with trucks, boats or smuggling. It suggested that I take the South Shore train that left Oakdale Station around noon, to change at Woodside for a train running on the branch line to West Egg station, where someone would pick me up.

My help was needed, the message read, on a "domestic matter." I reckoned Gatsby had not even made the call, but left the task to his servant, and wondered what he wanted from me.

Either way, I was excited to leave the cove. This was an off-day for the *Daisy*, as Wilson was taking down one of the ever-problematic Zenith carburetors. The company of my fellow train passengers—vacationers, shoppers, a few banker types leaving late for work; people other than my shipmates, or the glum, hope-starved crew of clam-diggers at the Dew Drop Inn—lifted my spirits.

So too did the sight of Gatsby standing beside his phaeton when I arrived at West Egg. I had assumed he would send his chauffeur. The fact that he had come in person now seemed, not very rationally and despite his earlier silence, an indication of my special status as friend rather than employee.

So did, of course, that profligate smile, the muscular clasp of hands. "We should have spent time together after that party," he said as we drove, "you must come to another—" We narrowly missed a Model T, loaded with chickens, coming the other way around a curve.

"I can't tell you, old sport," he cried after regaining control of the car, "how crucial you have been to this whole outfit. My boat, the *Daisy*—hell, do you know I would give my eye teeth to do a run with you? Though Meyer, of course, is opposed ..."

He drove fast, the way he usually did, and spoke louder than was necessary to make himself heard over the rush of wind and motor. While his hands were, as always, in motion—even when driving they adopted a suite of angles around his wrists—the one that was not on the wheel seemed more active than I remembered, repeatedly tapping his knee, flicking something invisible off the windshield, readjusting his hat. I recalled my first impression of him when we met at the Metropole: the sense that, over and above his usual drive, an extra package of energy ran inside him, like the third Liberty that sped up our rum-runner. Today I thought his extra energy had multiplied in force so much he could barely contain it with everyday business and behavior.

"The fact is"—he looked at me sideways—"I require you for another of your many skills." By now we had reached the postern at the entrance to his estate, but he continued more slowly down the road for another couple of hundred yards, stopping his car on the verge before a rutted dirt drive. He turned to face me full-on, bending slightly in my direction, punching the gear lever with one clenched fist.

"You see, old sport, I'm courting. Have been for a while. This girl—I've been in love with her since the war."

Buchanan's wife, I thought, but did not say it.

"She loves me too, I am as certain of that as I am of the sun rising tomorrow. She has, since then—but she—she has a child. I—" He looked away, then back at me. "She is everything to me, it's why—"

I stared at him in wonder. If there was one thing I would never have expected of Jay Gatsby, it was that he might leave a sentence unfinished.

"Anyway." He straightened, stared down the dirt drive. "Here's the job. My neighbor has agreed to throw a little tea party, and he will invite her to it, *and* me, so we can at last—officially—meet again. Do you see? Her name's Daisy, by the way—" He grinned. "You understand now, why the boat ..." The grin faded. "But he only has one maid—" Gatsby stated this as if it were an extraordinary deficiency that anyone could commiserate with—"and she is Finnish. She can cook, apparently, but she has almost no English, so—"

"So you want me to translate," I finished for him.

He nodded. "Exactly. I remembered you spoke the polly-voo. Just translate what we would need for a proper tea. Can you do that, old sport? Cakes, scones, certain jams ..." I nodded, and he drove us down the drive, to a summer cottage held hostage by a rabble of lawn. An old Dodge stood in an open shed to one side. Through cedars to the right I caught a glimpse of three gambrels on Gatsby's castle. A man came out of the cottage door and, though he was dressed only in cotton shirt and slacks, I recognized the flannel-clad friend of Jordan's from the party. He held a list in one hand—the items Gatsby wanted me to translate—and led me to the kitchen.

"Mrs. Korpi," he said, "this is Mister—" He looked at me.

"Laine," I said, using "Laï-*ee*-nay," the Finnish pronunciation.

Mrs. Korpi was sitting at a tin-topped table, watching her hands peel potatoes, but when I spoke she looked up, startled. She was a smallish woman in her late forties, or early sixties, it was hard to tell; her wrinkles seemed carved by care as much as by age. She was broad rather than stout, with graying hair yanked back in a bun, and cheekbones set well apart under slightly tilted brown eyes that spoke of Lapland blood, eyebrows and lips locked in a mild scowl; but when I spoke further in her own tongue they loosened and opened, in astonishment rather than pleasure. One had the immediate sense, on observing her, that pleasure was a sensation she had not experienced in a long time.

"I'll leave you to it, then," said the flannel-man; he had been introduced to me as Carraway. "Make sure she gets the pound cake straight, at least." I heard him talking to Gatsby in the sitting-room as I sat down. "If it's really inedible," he said, "I can get lemon cakes from the deli, but …" His voice trailed off as they walked outside.

Mrs. Korpi and I went through the list together. I couldn't translate many of the delicacies Gatsby had specified. Though my parents had spoken mostly Finnish while Eiki and I were growing up, what I knew was conversational and basic. The last time I'd spoken it was in Finn Town, and then only to argue with my landlady or order gin at Virtanens', so even that was rusty. "Pound cake," for example, and "scone" had to be described by what I knew of their ingredients and what I found in a very general cookbook that lay, dusty from disuse, on a nearby shelf. Mrs. Korpi penciled notes in the back of a small Lutheran hymnal, nodding as she jotted down the Suomi words, asking the occasional question about types of shortening or flour. When we had gone through the list I rose to leave, and her expression changed from stubborn concentration to one that almost approached panic; and I hesitated.

"Is there anything else I can do for you, *Rouva* Korpi?" I asked.

"Please," she said, "I didn't offer you anything."

"That's—"

"Would *Herra* Laine like coffee?"

"I don't need—" I wanted to get back to Gatsby. I was worried he would leave, that surplus of energy driving him to deal with whatever activity, financial or sentimental, awaited him next; he might already have arranged with Carraway to return me to the station. But her expression had changed back, from near-panic to an anticipatory sadness, and I relented.

"Of course," I said. "That would be kind."

She got up to boil water. And then she started talking, and for some time she did not stop. It felt like the breaking of a verbal dam, which for a Finn was sure sign of vast emotion. Her name was Adda, she told me, and she had no one else to converse with.

"My English, I know almost none. There are no Finns in this place." (She said this as a farmer might say "This land has no water.") "I came with my husband, he had a job in Vest-hampton, but he died of heart illness. I have only this job and it is not enough.…

Mister Carraway, he is not a bad man, I am sure, but he does not understand—"

She brought me the coffee pot and a cup, with cream and sugar in separate bowls, and a dense cardamom bun that both reminded me of home and explained why Carraway, and Gatsby, had desired my help. Still standing she said, "I don't understand him most of the time, so he gets angry, he thinks I am deliberately disobeying him, it makes everything worse."

"You don't want coffee?" I asked and she stared at me as if I had said something lewd. "Please," I added, as if I were the host and she the guest, and pointed at the pot. She dusted her hands in her apron, glanced nervously at the sitting-room door. She fetched a second cup and sat down, with some hesitation, opposite me.

"Don't you know anyone else here?" I asked, pouring.

She had a friend in Chicago, Mrs. Korpi told me, watching her coffee, and touched her face with a corner of the apron. I felt, all of a sudden, how immensely hard it must be, stuck in this village of aloof people and their summer castles, unable because of the language barrier to fulfill the menial role that was all she could aspire to. As if touched by a fairy wand it turned my frustration at being cooped up at the garage, or my sadness from the neglect I suffered at Jordan's hands, into things both puny and without merit.

"Your job with Mister Carraway—it's not full time? Not permanent?"

She shook her head.

"Can I—"

She looked up. The rims of her eyes were pink but she was too proud to wipe them again in front of me. I knew for certain that if I offered money to help her out she would refuse it.

"Would you like it," I said carefully, "if I asked *Heera* Gatsby next-door if he can give you extra work?"

She nodded: any work would be good. Mrs. Korpi wanted to earn enough money to buy her passage back to Finland, to a town called Oulu, where she still had family. She wished to see her homeland again, now that it was no longer occupied by Russians. I smiled at that; she uttered the word "Russians" the way my father used to, the way Mike said "*Turkiye*," and "*Rosia*" as well, like a curse.

I left her then, and went to the sitting room to find Gatsby gone, as I'd half-expected. Carraway was still there, and he handed me a note from my friend apologizing for having to leave early; inviting me, by way of apology, to a "special" party.

"Call my butler on Fridays," the note read. "He'll tell you when he has the date. I'll square it with MW." I wondered vaguely if Gatsby threw parties to make up for his absence or unavailability to others. Carraway let one of those vague, waiting-for-something-to-surprise-me smirks drift across his face as I pocketed the note; and said he would drive me to the station.

Which he did, after casting about for driving gloves. This took him several minutes of clumping around an upstairs room, leaving me free to peer through the open windows at Gatsby's place, and examine the books Carraway had on his shelves (the three-volume *Complete Guide to Securities*, by Ripley Snell; *Managing Your Trust Fund*, by Anthony Patch, Esq.; *Economics*, by Sir Henry Clay); and to notice, as I turned away from the bookshelves, a white scarf, decorated with a line of blue, inebriated dolphins, lying in a silken heap on the floor behind a wicker couch.

Chapter Eleven

The period that followed my visit to Carraway's was a time of greatly increased foreboding; of expecting a violence that never quite came or if it did, brushed close but did not actually hit. The New York headlines were black with assassination, one Sicilian gang always striving to kill members of another. In the most recent attempt a man named Masseria was ambushed by two men from the d'Aquila gang but escaped unhurt.

I thought Wolfshiem might telephone with further warnings, since he'd surmised d'Aquila's group were the ones trying to hijack the bootleg game in Queens, but no such warnings came.

The weather felt more ominous as well. Hurricanes were announced in the papers but they never strengthened, or else veered offshore well south of us. The only gifts such weather patterns sent were waves of increased humidity, sporadic rain, and heat.

Even in Tibbets' Cove the air grew thicker, more oppressive; it reminded me of Jordan's description of Louisville, where everything felt heavy, hard to move. The mosquitoes seemed to grow more voracious, and tempers frayed. Marcus snapped at everyone, which was unlike him. A couple of times at the Dew Drop he drank himself to the point of near-paralysis, and this also was unusual.

He missed his family, he confessed to me one night; he had the feeling Sarah was growing up without her father. Despite the money he was making he was of half a mind to quit.

Every Friday I telephoned Gatsby's house. Each time the butler told me Mr. Gatsby had no party scheduled for that weekend, or at least no party to which his employee, Mr. Laine, might be invited.

The runs we made were welcome, despite the government cutters—which were now patrolling the coast with greater diligence—despite the ever-present danger the shoals off Fire Island Inlet represented for our delicate craft. Al Tibbets had shown me the bearings to take (on a yellow barn, the inlet's eastern tip, a hill) so I could pilot us in and out on my own, but the channel was still narrow and shallow, and any kind of onshore breeze churned up the surf. My chest felt like it filled with spiders every time we had to cross. Still, it also felt good to leave the cove and its mosquitoes, and once we were offshore the ocean gave us relief from the heat.

Ocean or no ocean, though, what had at first seemed a welcome holiday from the Land of Ashes, a furlough with good pay and clean air, after a month of this existence had been baked, dragged out and mildewed into a seemingly endless stretch of marsh stink and rough gin, and a bizarre form of shared solitude among the *Daisy's* crew. So that when it finally came to an end, on a soggy evening in mid-August; though it finished in a manner that warned of tragedy to come, none of us were particularly sorry.

It happened this way. I was sitting in the back room of the Dew Drop, drinking whisky with Wilson and Marcus. In the bar nextdoor a couple of local men were arguing with Conklin over the migratory habits of bluefish. Marcus had already called Wolfshiem's office to tell him the tide and weather looked favorable for a run tomorrow and to schedule a pickup at the barn that evening.

Wilson had finally got the exhaust bypass working again. He was downing a drink before driving back to the garage. He was in a bad mood, which was hardly new—because of Myrtle, which also was not a surprise.

"We always talk about moving," he told us gloomily. "Like I said, all she wanted was to go back to the city, but once we got here she wanted to move out West, *not* Detroit—California or Oregon I guess, she always says the West is clean, ya know, it's new … And now I'm sayin' yeah, okay, maybe we should try that—an', an' she just ignores me. Or she looks at me like she wishes I would disappear."

Marcus shook his head. I was about to say something along the lines of how going out West might be a great idea for both of them when the next-door room fell silent. This, we had learned, was a sign that someone Conklin didn't know had entered the bar.

After a little while a new voice asked a question, and was met with further silence. I got up and pressed my ear to one of the wider chinks in the uneven pine boards that formed the Dew Drop's walls.

"… new boat in this area, like a yacht, fancy like that," the newcomer was saying. "White painted. Bottle-fishin'." It was a man's voice, fairly high, more like a loud whisper in which the sibilants were pulled long, as in a snake's hiss. And it had accent in it, very light, like a drop of claret in a glass of water.

"You a cop?" Conklin asked.

The man laughed. It was not a pleasant sound, it was full of contempt and a promise of, even a taste for, violence. I angled my head to peer through the chink. I had to press the left side of my face against the rough pine, risking splinters to find an angle that would let me view that stretch of bar; even then I could not see much. Conklin was invisible. I was half-expecting the short fat man with hooded eyes and a dark coat whom Jordan and Wolfshiem had both mentioned, but what I could see of the speaker looked different: a thin, fairly tall shape in a dark suit. His fedora was pulled low over his eyes, and in the lousy lighting that was part of the Dew Drop's dubious charm, the black shadows in eye sockets and cheekbones made his face look like that of a skull, or a ghost.

"I ain't a cop," he said. "Two, three guys," he added, "on the yacht? They run out to a steam freighter.… Here's a twenty to help you remember."

I could almost hear the calculator in Conklin's brain clicking away. He was not a man to refuse twenty bucks lightly, but we were paying him the same amount every day and the end result was a given.

"Ain't seen nothin' like that," he said finally. "'round here it's mostly fishing boats, locals. Try Westhampton, or Montauk."

"I'll do that," the skull-face said. He made it sound like a threat. And a few minutes later he was gone.

Chapter Twelve

Marcus phoned Wolfshiem as soon as the skull-faced man had left; with the result that by 6 a.m. the next morning, the *Daisy* and her crew were on our way back to Queens.

I have spoken before of the gambler's experience of hoping to win and hoping to win, and the more he hopes and the longer he keeps hoping, with an ever-increasing intensity and desperation, the more he seems to lose; until finally, flat broke or even owing more than he possesses, and persuaded that he is destined always to lose, he decides to quit the game forever—and how, at or near that moment, when he knows he will quit but through some technicality of poker must play out his final hand, he fills an inside straight.

I had this experience in mind when I got back to the garage after the long haul east to Montauk, then west to the Flushing River; when once more I drew in the infernal breath of the Land of Ashes, and heard the howl of dump dogs, and felt again the eyes of Dr. T.J. Eckleburg follow my every move; and saw the sun's face, scarlet from suffocation, drown in haze on a horizon of smoldering coke.

I was tired. We had stayed up late, getting *Daisy* ready for an early start, and what sleep we managed was broken by mosquitoes and the heat. And the run back, in greasy swells from the east that made the boat roll like a drunk on St. Croix Avenue, was tiring. But the sense of setback, of failure even, stemmed from more than fatigue.

I had noticed, when coming back from a trip: when I got home after *Tuolomee*, or from the Navy; how the shift from new and ever-changing experience to near-forgotten places and habits allowed you to see, as for the first time, how small and often rotted were the walks and occupations of your old existence. Standing at the side door to the warehouse I realized, and for the first time clearly, that a half-educated, Midwestern, rum-running skipper like me had as much hope of being loved by Jordan Baker as that family of dump-pickers had of finding the Koh-I-Noor among the charred clinker they fossicked in.

Moreover, as a man from the Midwest who had abandoned a family already shattered by loss to chase the easy lucre available out East, I hardly merited the attention of anyone worthwhile. The illusion to which I'd fallen victim at Gatsby's party—the fantasy that our shared myth of America would allow someone like me to enter the circle of the elegant and rich simply by virtue of a good suit, a ready smile and a desperate wish to be someone other than who he was—I now saw as the sham and baubled illusion it always had been. I was a man with no real friends other than the pals of convenience he made working on the water: a former shipmate whom Gatsby called when he needed him for a job, and ignored otherwise.

I had of course the Great American Consolation of money; and I remembered, with my usual vagueness of quote, what Marcus Aurelius wrote: "It is said of wealth ... if we should value and think those things to be good ... that he who hath them, through pure abundance, hath not a place to be at peace himself?"

I had not found peace. I had not even found a place to buy records by Ethel Waters or any other recordings of the new, exciting kind of jazz music I'd hoped to find in New York. If I heard another ragtime song on my Victrola, I thought, I would take the record, smash it, and throw the pieces out of Mike's coffeeshop into the dust.

When you sink this low all that is left is your body and its needs, to move and piss and eat. I unlocked the warehouse door, carried my duffel bag upstairs. The note tacked to my door, amid my

complete lack of hope, seemed perfectly neutral in value. I dropped
the duffel bag, ripped down the note—it was an uneven piece of
ruled paper, oil-stained, torn from an old accounts book—and read,
in George Wilson's clumsy hand:

> *Mr Gatsby Sed Come to W. Egg Saterday Nite Its O.K. With*
> *Mr Wolfsheem*

I read the note over, twice, three times. Given what I had been
thinking over the last few minutes, I could only assume Gatsby
had come up with another job for me to do; or else, because of the
mysterious fellow who had asked after us at the Dew Drop, because
Gatsby now had doubts about the safety of the Queens boathouse,
he wanted to discuss shifting the *Daisy's* base again.

I did not move. I kept looking at that scrap of paper, the way
I'd kept staring at the telegram in Duluth. And slowly, tentatively,
as if I had no control over them at all, my shoulders began to relax.
And my back, that had bent a little to one side from the weight of
my duffel bag, seemed to straighten, till I was standing upright once
more.

—

Like a dream whose details you don't remember but whose taste
and back-tune inhabit your mind, the sense of observing a familiar place with new eyes was still strong in me that Saturday night,
when for the second time that summer I came to Gatsby's.

The place had not changed physically, of course. A shower earlier in the day had cooled the air somewhat and licked up grass
around the tents. The sound of crickets and tree frogs seemed louder
than before and now a bullfrog, invisible in a marshland beyond the
lights, added his baritone to the refrain of chatter and music.

Otherwise it was as if I had slipped back through time to the
same party I'd attended earlier that summer: the graceful men in
straw boaters and summer suits, the women in dresses that were

daring and hats that sought to be, seemed to mingle, drink and sometimes dance to the identical flow and rhythm as before. The glowing windows of the château, the flicker of candles that spread like a migration of wights across the lawns and terraces, seemed as familiar as a painting hung in your room that you decided to hang elsewhere and so, for the first time in years, looked at again.

And at the same time it all seemed quite different, in ways I could not define.

For one thing I was not drinking French 75s. I took a flute of champagne from a passing waiter and sipped at it slowly as I walked. Perhaps because I was not drinking as hard, the people around me seemed more inebriated, more obsessed, more extreme in their pursuit of whatever they had come here to chase: women or men, escape or financial connections, or the lily-swipe of fame's proximity. On a wrought-iron bench under a gnarled fruit tree, illuminated as on a stage by a cluster of lamps, I saw a woman whose perfectly shaped nose and tiny mouth, framed by a thicket of artfully disarranged locks, were as familiar to me and to millions of picture-show viewers as the faces of our mothers.

The man with the shovel-shaped chin, leaning in so close as to be almost kissing her, was nearly as famous as Lillian Gish. Amid this cloud of strange familiarity the presence of people known by the light they projected on a screen seemed quite normal.

What was not expected, or rather what I had not formulated or recognized till now, was that I was no longer as concerned with seeing Jordan Baker. The thought of her, like the reverberation of a bell struck earlier, still summoned a note of longing within me; but it was lesser, I thought and prayed, compared to the tumult and rush that once had engulfed my being. And in the accounting books of desire this dip in value seemed balanced by a new accessibility. While at the last party I'd spent hours circling in search of her, tonight I came upon Jordan within ten minutes of my arrival—Jordan and Gatsby, along with Tom Buchanan, Carraway the flannel man, and a small, blond woman, all strolling around the lawns so slowly as to seem immobile.

"Jon!" Gatsby called, and waved me into their group. His smile, as always, raised me to the social equivalent of visiting royalty; and he introduced me, as "my friend from olden days, Mister Laine," to "Mister Buchanan the famous polo player, and his wife the lovely Daisy Buchanan"—who leaned forward to peer at me as if fascinated by something on my nose and murmured, in a throbbing voice, that she was both thrilled and infinitely delighted to make my acquaintance.

I observed with interest the namesake of my boat, the woman my friend was in love with despite her being married—despite (I remembered now) the presence of a child. She was not as beautiful as I had expected: her mouth, though prettily bowed, was perhaps a bit too small, her green eyes set apart to match her forehead but not the rest; her nose had a tiny indentation at the tip. Her hair, of the same milky gold as Jordan's, was cut slightly shorter than her friend's, which did nothing to offset a sharp jawline. The intensity of her appearance held a tinge of being out of control, like a biplane whose pilot had parachuted to safety and was left to circle, roll, change altitude and direction at the behest of wind and its own tendencies, so that you could not keep yourself from watching to see where it would crash.

"And what do y'all *do*, Mister Laine?" she asked me in those same throbbing tones, and when Gatsby interjected quickly, "Mister Laine is in the shipping business," proclaimed that this was just tremendously exciting because she so longed to board a gorgeous ship for ports unknown, as she and Tom had once done to go to France. Her enthusiasm was so extreme that, paradoxically, it felt quite hopeless—like a quip uttered by someone badly wounded, just prior to surgery.

We continued strolling as a loose group, with the occasional acquaintance hailed in passing. Gatsby walked beside Daisy and talked to her in a voice no one else could overhear. Buchanan prowled restlessly, drawing ahead then glancing at his wife and Gatsby and circling back to the group. It seemed clear to me, in my un-drunk state, that the physical closeness of Gatsby and his wife bothered him not a little; and I took a small, mean pleasure in the revenge fate was exacting on Wilson's behalf.

I had been walking on the other side of our group from Jordan, trying not to look at her as she half-loped in her loose, sporty fashion alongside Carraway, but I could not help noticing the way her hips filled the thin white dress she wore; a dress, I noticed, that was the twin of Daisy Buchanan's and which together with their similar hair—of the same color, as I'd already noted, and cut in the French bob fashionable at the time—evoked a vague notion of sisterhood. But when Daisy, with a cry of delight, ran to a nearby table and embraced another woman sitting there; when, urged to join that group, we were introduced ("the polo player; the shipping man") and took spare chairs around the table; Jordan chose the seat next to mine and asked at once, "Are you avoiding me, Jon?"

I looked at her: the head-thrown study of my face; the lips that had once touched mine; the gray eyes that looked into my own so deeply, at the Metropole, when we lay together … She was wearing the dolphin scarf I had last seen, abandoned, on Carraway's floor.

"It's the other way around," I said, "isn't it?"

"Is it?" she said, as if the idea were completely new to her, then sighed. "Ah s'pose …"

The woman Daisy had embraced, an attractive, gum-chewing blonde in a blue dress, was talking loudly. "Everybody has wings in this city," she cried, "ah can feel the brush of them against mah arms as we are walking in the street." She had an accent like Jordan's, and I looked at the woman beside me as if to check for other resemblance. I had no chance with Jordan, I reminded myself, but my heart sped up all the same when she touched my hand with hers, and my breath hesitated as it had before.

"Ah'm with someone now," Jordan said. "We may get married." Still studying my face. "Ah hope you and I can still be friends."

Friends, I thought bitterly: the noun that in a romantic context was equivalent to the sentence, "I order the defendant to be taken from here to a place of execution and hung by the neck until dead." I felt again the despair I'd known at Tibbets' Cove, where it had pulled me down as if someone set concrete around my ankles. But it had lost some heft compared to before, and I saw in that subtraction a navigable hope, that someday I could remember her and not hurt.

I jerked my chin toward Carraway.

"Is it him?"

She laughed, too loud as always.

"Oh lordy no. Not Nick. He's in love with someone else."

"But I thought he and you—"

"Be serious, Jon. Just open your eyes—" She pointed at the flannel man. "See who he's looking at."

I looked. The Southern woman who felt angel wings, and her husband who was even prettier and more dramatic than his wife—he had been introduced as "the famous novelist from Great Neck"—were telling a funny story to Daisy, who was laughing well before the punch line. Carraway's head was tilted that way to listen, but his eyes were fixed on Gatsby.

"You mean," I said incredulously.

"What do *you* think?"

"You mean?"

She nodded. "He just doesn't know it yet. Nor does Jay."

"But doesn't he—I mean, Jay's not—What I'm saying, Jay's completely loopy over your friend."

"Is he?"

"Of course he is. Look at what *he's* looking at."

She smiled, now peering at Gatsby. "Well, maybe what Jay really loves is the whole package. The beautiful woman, the endless money, the assumption of permanence—isn't that what all con artists desire deep down? Something permanent?"

"Jay's not a con artist."

"Really? I thought all you yankees were."

I got up then. My glass was empty. Just like last time I offered to fetch Jordan a drink but her glass was, as always, half-full. I found a dark-skinned waiter circling nearby with a tray full of cocktails, of an alarming shade of orange, that he said were called "Ward

Eights." I grabbed one and drained that drink a lot faster than I'd drunk the champagne. It was a whisky drink, only half-sweet; I liked it better than the French 75s I'd guzzled last time.

When I rejoined the table Daisy was eyeing the same waiter, who was giving away the last of his tray of cocktails, and saying that Tom was right, something had to be done before the "colored races" submerged us all. The low and thrilling tone in which she uttered this opinion gave it the weight and portent of a Delphic prophecy. Her husband, seizing the opportunity to draw his wife's attention, said forcefully: "What we need is to go back to how things were, before this modernism and jazz!" And the writer's wife, trying perhaps to restore levity to the conversation, pointed past the swimming pool, down the forty-acre lawn, to the line of sea visible outside Gatsby's little bay where, beyond a gas buoy, the red portlight and white steaming lights of a westbound freighter shone like semi-precious stones in the humid air.

Look," she cried, "is that one of your boats?"

I realized she was looking up at me—I had not yet sat down.

"No," I said, but she had everyone's attention by then. Her gestures and voice were loose with liquor. In her the looseness was attractive.

"Ah'd lahk to be a boat lahk that," she said in a sighing sort of voice, "sailing against the current, borne back ceaselessly into the past."

No one had an answer to that, and after a pause I remarked, "Well, it's Long Island Sound, and the current reverses every six hours, roughly, so it would just take you back to the present." At this everybody laughed, which made me feel, for a few seconds, witty and accepted.

A different waiter, this one a member of the threatened white races, appeared behind Gatsby and whispered something in his ear which caused him to nod, stand, and address the table. "Please excuse me," he said, "I am called to the office, something urgent," and as he left waved at me to accompany him. I got up and left the table without looking at or saying another word to Jordan.

"So what do you think, old sport?" he asked as we walked swiftly toward the house.

"About what?"

"You know exactly, about what." Gatsby's left fist was clenched; he put his right arm around my shoulders. I had the usual gut reaction to his intimate manner, and to his voice, which was as rich on the male scale as Daisy Buchanan's was on the female; I wondered if this commonality had anything to do with their attraction to each other. But beyond that familiar sense of being uniquely flattered and trusted by him I detected, even more strongly, the supplemental energy I had felt from the day we renewed acquaintance at the Metropole—and at last understood, by the proximity of its source, where he drew it from.

"She's pretty," I said and, instinctively seeking to lower the octane of our discourse, added, "All these Southern girls, they—"

"She's going to leave him." Now he stopped, forcing me to stop with him, and looked intently into my eyes. We were near the orchestra, which was playing a waltz, and he spoke louder to make himself heard. "We're going to leave together. I wanted you to meet her first."

"I—I'm glad I did."

He put both his hands on my shoulders now and gave me a shake, as if physically to jiggle me out of whatever doubts I might have about his plan.

"She makes everything around me, I don't know, it feels as if the whole world is the most wonderful buffet, a thousand times better than this"—he swept a hand at the two-dozen buffet tables before returning it to my shoulder—"the most light and excellent drink and sweetmeats you can imagine, and all I want is to gobble and drink it all up and then do it again, and again—all my life."

He was still gazing into my eyes, still gripping my shoulders, and now he gripped harder.

"You may not realize it, Jon—you're the oldest friend I have around here. Anywhere, really. These people—" He glanced around him. "Most of them I don't even know, they just show up. And the rest—"

He shook his head as if perplexed by what he himself was saying.

"You're the link—the *one link* I have between who I was, and who I am now. Do you understand?"

I didn't really, but I nodded anyway. He nodded, dropped his gaze, let go of my shoulders, and we resumed our march up the various steps and terraces to the château; through a maze of hallways, salons; past the same piano-player, tinkling at the Bechstein; to a study in which Wolfshiem and his niece stood reading a newspaper, looking temporary, as if they weren't sure where they'd ended up and were just waiting to leave.

Wolfshiem turned as soon as we walked in.

"You seen this?" he cried, brandishing the newspaper.

Gatsby took the paper. Stella smiled at me, her smile that lifted one corner of the mouth higher than the other. She was dressed in sober colors compared to the women outside but her dress was as short and her legs as fine as any of theirs. Her smile was fresh, un-drunk and warm.

"How are you, Mister Laine?" she asked quietly, and I smiled back. Jay turned and thrust the paper at me, pointing to a headline under the fold. "'The Ghost' Murdered," it read. "Umberto Valente, Wanted Assassin, Shot at 12th Street Restaurant."

A rotogravure image was printed over the headlines. It showed a thin man in a dark suit and fedora, with sunken cheeks and eyes inhabiting a long, contemptuous face. The picture was blurry but how the shadows haunted the man's skeletal features evoked in me a dyspeptic twinge of recognition.

"Is that him?" Gatsby asked.

"The man you saw in Oakdale," Wolfshiem added from close beside me. The hairs that sprouted from his nose seemed to have grown longer: they quivered with the tension inside.

"It sure looks like him," I said, and Wolfshiem frowned.

"That's *good* news, Meyer," Gatsby told him, folding the news-paper. "This says he's d'Aquila's goon. So it had to be Masseria's guys who killed him—and Masseria's with *us*."

"It buys us time, is all." Wolfshiem's cigar had gone out. He opened a box of matches and lit it again. "His boss is still out there: Mineo." He blew smoke at the ceiling. "What I wanna know is, who blabbed? Who of our people told him where the boat was?"

"They didn't know exactly," Gatsby pointed out. "Anyway, this is one big reason I wanted to keep the boats separate—"

"We got rid of the first captain," Wolfshiem interrupted, jerking his chin toward me, "'cause he was shooting his mouth off. What about you," and now he looked more directly at me than he ever had before. "Did *you* talk?"

"Jon doesn't talk," Gatsby said, frowning. "He's Finnish, you can leave him alone."

"Huh," Wolfshiem grunted. He didn't sound convinced. "I don't trust those Italians," he continued, still looking near me, but then averted his gaze, presumably because I didn't look Italian. "There's too much blood, vendettas, it goes back to their villages. You never know who's gonna go after who next. My people—"

Gatsby lit a cigarette, offered me one.

"Your people?"

"Yeah, *my* people." Wolfshiem glanced toward Stella. "Katspaugh, Lansky's bunch. This new kid, Flegenheimer. They don't have feuds, not that kind. And they don't blab." Now he blew smoke at the newspaper. "It's all business, with them. You know where you stand, with business."

They kept talking in lower voices, which I presumed meant I was not supposed to hear, though I heard "Mineo" repeated twice, and Wolfshiem saying "he's trickier, what you can expect from him is what you *don't* expect." I walked over to Stella, who was standing by the French windows, smoking, parting the drapes with one hand to watch the party outside.

"How's your lady friend?" she asked, not looking at me.

"Engaged."

She looked at me then.

"To you?"

I smiled, and she smiled, and in our smiles lived the truth I had but recently accepted, that girls like Jordan did not end up with fellows like me. The orchestra moved into a slower tune, a waltz I knew called "Three o'clock in the morning." Her attention was drawn outside again and her smile now seemed wistful, and without thinking I asked, "Would you care to dance with me?"

She stared at me now. Flicked ash out the window. "I—"

It was the first time I'd seen her look anything but cool, or sarcastic.

"Come on," I urged. "It's just a dance."

She glanced at Wolfshiem, who was still huddled with Gatsby. "I'm not really s'posed to."

"Well, don't tell him." Suddenly the favor I wished for most, from heaven or fate or the devil, was to take this thin sarcastic creature in my arms and dance her down the canvas to the strains of a popular song. "Tell him we're just going to get a drink."

Those night-dyed pupils were full of reflected smoke, and doubt; tonight they seemed less dark than I'd once thought, almost hazel in places, with threads of emerald among the somber colors that only added to their message of uncertainty. But she stubbed out her cigarette in a nearby ashtray and said something to Wolfshiem, who waved his hand as he continued talking in a low voice to Gatsby.

We found our way out, to the tent that sheltered the dance floor. The orchestra played beside, light bouncing and splashing on the brass instruments the way it had, so long ago it seemed, at Edmond's Cellar. I looked around for Jordan, uncertain whether or not I wished for her to see me dance with Stella. On balance, I thought, I'd rather she didn't; she would not look jealous, and I'd prefer to avoid measuring from that the fathomless nature of her indifference.

But Stella was looking up at me, doubtful again, and the waltz was halfway done. I put an arm around her waist and clasped her hand in the other. We needed to dance now, while a waltz was playing.

Stella Wolfshiem and I began to move, and circle, and twirl around the other dancers, across the canvas floor.

———

It should have been the perfect ending to the night, but perfect endings are rare outside cheap novels. I wanted to quit the party after I escorted Stella back to the study so as to wind up, relatively sober, clear-headed and not too late, in my own bed over the warehouse; but when I asked Wolfshiem if he could drop me off on his way to the city, Gatsby interrupted and requested that I stay.

He was in his over-intense mood again, only more so. Once our co-conspirators had left he ranged back and forth across the study like a caged coyote. He dug out a bottle of Haig, poured me a glass and talked, without pause, about Daisy and how she had never loved her husband and how he had fallen in love with her years ago, long before she met Tom, when Gatsby was in the Army and stationed outside Louisville. Then, as if a light switch had flipped, he said, "I have to go," and strode for the door.

He stopped, and half-turned back.

"I meant it, about joining you for that run, old sport," he said quietly. "Once more at sea, eh? The way we used to be on *Tuolomee*." And then added: "I'll come next time. That's a promise."

His talk of smuggling runs reminded me of the *Daisy*'s first captain, the one he and Wolfshiem had "got rid of," which I'd meant to ask him about; but by the time I formed the question he had gone.

Later, when I went outside, I saw him at the table with Daisy, Tom Buchanan and the flannel man. Daisy and Gatsby were talking, their heads close together, while Buchanan listened to Carraway. I had not the slightest desire to join them.

I walked toward the water as I had last time, only alone. What was it about the sea, I wondered idly—even its milquetoast approximation in Long Island Sound—that drew me, and not just me but others too? Was it simply a flat shiny surface on which we could project our dreams, the way a projector screened our fantasies? Or was it something more fundamental: a vast, mysterious power that jolted us out of our sidewalk concerns of sham and money to remind us, briefly, of how insignificant and short was our time on Earth?

The air had cooled further. It had a tiny bite to it, like mouse-teeth in the breeze, that carried a premonition of dying leaves, of fall. I was grateful to be wearing a full suit; I buttoned up the jacket and walked on. Despite my vague musings, despite the whisky Gatsby had served, I still felt clear-headed.

In this I was anomalous. I walked past a woman in a crêpe de chine dress and silk jacket who sat next to the statue of a mermaid, sobbing quietly, as if she and the mermaid had both just gone through something awful together. Past two men, one in white knickerbockers, trying to fight behind a hedge. "Bastard!" they yelled at each other. "You *bas*-tard!" Both were so tight that each time one swung a fist he overbalanced and fell without touching the other.

From behind a hedge a disembodied voice called "Duckweed! Where, oh where's, my *tiara*?"

As always, the wait-staff trudged among the half-eaten plates of food, the empty glasses, the unconscious guests—like stretcher-bearers at Manassas slowly bearing dead boys away. I barely noticed them now; they all wore the same uniform and walked as if trying to both serve and hide, but as I passed a woman carrying a vast basket filled with dirty china, something about her width and facial shape made me take a second look.

"*Rouva* Korpi?" I ventured.

She stopped.

"*Herra* Laine?"

She was holding the basket with both arms, legs braced.

"So you got a job here. I'm glad." I looked more closely at the basket, which held several dozen plates and must have weighed at least forty pounds. "That's heavy, isn't it?"

"It's fine."

"They shouldn't ask you to carry so much."

"It's fine, *Herra* Laine," she said impatiently. "I thank you for your help but I must go." And she stumped off, legs set widely to keep her balance, toward a cart wheeled by another shape in black and white.

After watching her go I resumed my own walk and eventually came to the beach. A thin fog was forming on Long Island Sound, and far away a foghorn lowed, but a rich belt of stars spread a verse of silver from above, and across the little bay the same green light shone, its reflection stuttering across the ripples. It reminded me of the green lantern on *Loch Alsh*, but held no other signal for me.

No one else was on the beach. Far away, the orchestra still played dance tunes.

I watched the water. It appeared, in its darkness, at once conspiratorial and soft. The light breeze touched me where I stood in my fine suit and shoes and hat.

I took off my clothes, dropped them where I stood, and walked into the cool forgiving sea.

Ward Eight

ingredients

2 oz. Scotch whisky
1/2 ounce fresh lemon juice, strained
1/2 ounce fresh orange juice
1/4 ounce grenadine
splash of seltzer

instructions

Shake everything but seltzer in ice-filled mixing tin
Strain into chilled glass
Add seltzer to taste

Chapter Thirteen

I didn't know it then—nor, I believe, did Gatsby—but that was the last party he would ever throw in West Egg. I wasn't sure if this was entirely Jay's decision, or Wolfshiem's. Whether or not someone in our operation had "blabbed" it made sense to keep our heads low following The Ghost's inquiries at the Dew Drop Inn; and though Valente had been killed shortly afterwards, the threat he represented lived on.

Still, as far as we knew, Mineo had not found the garage. Most of us now figured the danger was past, lost amid the daily churn of South Italian quarrels.

Whatever the reasons, a few days after that last party Gatsby fired his entire staff—including, I feared, Mrs. Korpi—and hired a crew made up only of Wolfshiem people. Two more goons were assigned to protect the depot and garage area. One of them, to Mike's delight, turned out to be both a poker lover, and an even lousier player than George Wilson.

For a long time we made no further runs. *Daisy* waited, idle if well-maintained, in the moldy dusk of the Flushing River boathouse. The *Loch Alsh*, finally emptied of her low-rent hootch, sailed back to St. Pierre for another cargo. Days passed, then weeks, and neither she nor her unlucky sister ship returned.

A cold front moved in for three days to break the heat. The sky, where we could see it through the dump smoke, seemed so bright and blue you felt it would squeak if you polished it with one of Mike's dishrags.

The feeling that crisp air brought, of summer coming to an end, reminded me of home. For many people this would have been a bittersweet idea, but I had always liked the approach of autumn weather. Maybe it was the Finn in me—certainly it was the Minnesotan—but summer always felt unnatural: welcome of course, and vital for our senses to break out of wool clothes and heated rooms into a profligacy of milkweed and birdsong, of warm sun on bare skin; but also, at its heart, a scam. Real seasons were built of cold and ice, the true work was surviving them, the real celebrations when you had finished the job and could rest with friends around a birch fire and drink and tell each other lies about everything you would do when the ice broke.

Maybe because of those feelings I finally put a call through to Uncle Tai. He did not sound pleased to get my call but said my parents were OK, no thanks to their surviving son. That was all I wanted to hear. I asked Tai to tell them I was fine and still in New York, and hung up, feeling relieved of a burden I'd forgotten that I bore.

Gatsby didn't call, despite what he'd promised about participating in a run. This did not surprise me, given his baroque romantic plans, and I wondered if the run he'd really had in mind was to flee with Daisy, and if he'd even let me know when that occurred.

I called his house twice and the man who answered told me, in unvarnished Brooklynese, that Gatsby was not around and no, he didn't know where he was and wouldn't later, either.

A couple of times I called Wolfshiem's office, ostensibly to ask for news of Gatsby but really to speak to Stella, the memory of whose smile and waist had simmered into a mental stew of waltz and starshine that slopped into my brain when I had trouble sleeping.

So, less happily, did thoughts of Jordan. Stella always sounded happy to talk but the one time I got leave to come into town, and invited her out for lunch, she said she was not free and frankly in all likelihood never would be.

I had a good enough time in the city to ban her from my thoughts that day. Like any other Midwestern tourist I walked Fifth Avenue gawking at the shop-windows and skyscrapers. I liked the feel of Manhattan on a hot afternoon: fewer people walked the streets, and those that did were mostly locals, and looked at each other through sweat-stung eyes with half-concealed empathy, as if to acknowledge for the first time what it took to survive here, and how the game might not be worth the candle.

I ate in a restaurant where a quarter bought you a meal served, to all appearances, by a wall of shined-up machines. The real object of my trip was a music store on 43rd Street where I purchased the single Ethel Waters record they had in stock, plus a dozen other discs the salesman said contained similar music: songs from people named Bessie Smith, Alberta Hunter, James Price Johnson. I also purchased a brand-new recording of Fats Waller, who I remembered had been the piano player at Edmond's Cellar.

I brought them all to Mike's and spent hours drinking coffee or "English Tea" and listening to those records, in particular the four or five songs that included "blues" in their titles, and which contained the stretched, cat-lithe rhythms I'd heard that night in Edmond's. The music made me happy, and helped to lighten the mood of others.

Marcus had cheered right up as soon as he got back and was able to see Essie-Mae and Sarah, but now it was Mike's turn to enter a period of despair. The resupplied Turkish army had, at the end of August, launched an assault on Greek positions in Asia Minor. A battle in a place called Dumlupinar ended with the Greeks in full retreat and Smyrna besieged and burning. Every morning the newspapers included another grim dispatch, another Hellenic setback, and the cries of "*Gamoto!*" and "*Turkiye!*," along with the crash of banging pots, filled our little diner. Stavros typically showed up around the time Mike brought back the papers, and he got more upset than Mike; he had relatives in Smyrna. He even stopped pulling the occasional transient into a game of thimblerig, as usually happened whenever Mike was not looking. Instead the two Greeks sat for hours, for days, talking with their heads together in tones that suggested mayhem, plot, revenge.

For a while Wilson, like Marcus, was an exception to the reign of gloom at Mike's. Thanks to the hapless guard, he occasionally won at poker; and from the smile that squatted his lips as a result you would have thought his troubles and even the troubles of all New York City had magically disappeared. I had not seen Tom Buchanan at the garage since he brought Myrtle and me to Manhattan, and while I wasn't sure if that meant Myrtle had given up her fancy man, the few times I glimpsed the Wilsons together they seemed friendly enough.

That state of affairs lasted till the morning he banged into the coffeeshop, fists clenched and cheeks puce with fury, and demanded that Mike confess what he had been doing with Myrtle the previous evening.

Mike had just read about the surrender of an entire Greek brigade. He was in no mood for mollifying jealous husbands and told Wilson to scram, and when Wilson went for him both he and Stavros drew knives. Wilson left, yelling that he would come back with his gun, but sensibly did not return.

They talked it out later, but from then on George Wilson's mood was grim. He long ago had sold the last flivver on his lot and now muttered ceaselessly about making big money on that barely used Ford; this, along with what he was now winning at poker, would finally allow him and Myrtle to move West. I remembered then the blue car Buchanan wished to sell.

Tom Buchanan did not show, however, and as the days passed Wilson grew even paler than usual, except for the circles that bloomed darker under his eyes. He shuffled around like a prisoner of war. Mike, who didn't hold a grudge except with Turks, watched him darkly. "In Greece it is goddesses who is the most jealous," he told me, as Wilson sat bowed over an English Tea one afternoon, "but in this man"—he jerked his chin at Wilson—"it is so strong like in Hera. If he can only use this, this thing he has—ga-MO-to!" He searched for the word, mangling a dishtowel in his hands.

"Force?" I suggested. "Feeling?"

"Force, yes—if he can use this force for himself, he can make, you know—*gamoto*."

I didn't learn what Wilson might make, as Mike couldn't find the words he needed, and took out his frustration on the stove-top grease.

I should have been morose as well; or rather, the man I used to be would have felt at home in the gloom at Mike's. A compromise settlement of the railroad strike had fallen through and the National Guard was called out in several states to protect scabs and bust picket lines. A judge in the pocket of railroad companies outlawed the strike; President Harding's attorney general, a union-hater named Daugherty, had the leaders arrested: and the Great Railroad Strike of 1922 was over.

The news elicited in me a flick of anger, a habit of outrage and sympathy, that lasted a couple of days. But I continually reminded myself of what I'd learned about my country, about what Gatsby had understood from the first when he signed on to *Tuolomee*: that power was on the side of money, and Americans would go along with any trick or scam if it got them rich. I fingered the ever-growing roll of cash in my pocket, wound up the gramophone, ordered an English Tea, and thought of other things.

And then, on a day toward the middle of September when nothing particularly new had happened in the world; when summer, determined not to give up without a fight, had wrapped New York City in what would prove to be the last and most intense heat wave of the year; everything changed, once more.

—

That morning, Wilson shuffled to Mike's with the news that the *Loch Alsh* was due in Long Island Sound the following night. It was short notice again, but I figured this was now a deliberate move on the part of our bosses, to reduce the chances of a snitch in their operation leaking information to d'Aquila's bunch. A warm front spinning twenty-five-knot southwesterlies had blown in the day before, but had since moved offshore; the wind was diminishing, Long Island Sound would be calm enough tomorrow for our rendezvous.

We were to get the *Daisy* ready this evening, Wilson announced, and sleep aboard, then move to Port Jefferson inlet at dawn tomorrow and anchor there to wait.

All this we did, though Young Sam was late getting to the boathouse next morning, so we did not leave as early as we were supposed to. The Farting Studey had given him trouble, Young Sam claimed, handing me a greasy package of blinis still warm from the oven—it was a bribe a blind saint could see through—but he gave us his reluctant, pimply smile while saying this, so neither Marcus nor I could get too angry with him.

"My cousin said you liked these," he said as he unwrapped the blinis, and I thought of Stella with a bouquet of affection, along with a sprig of annoyance for thinking kindly of Jon Laine while keeping him, always, at arm's length.

Young Sam had also brought a chart of the North Shore on which was marked a dock where we were to tie up in Port Jefferson while waiting for tonight's rendezvous: another change in our usual routine, to frustrate the snitch I supposed.

We chewed blinis as we cruised up the East River. We had almost finished the package when I noticed a black launch following us. It had an oddly rounded pilothouse. "Marcus," I said, "isn't that—?" He looked where I was pointing, mouth full; squinted, shrugged. I remembered that he'd been in the engine room for the early part of our first run. "Whoever he is, we can do twice his speed," Marcus said, and disappeared down the engine room hatch. Young Sam was standing beside me and on impulse I told him, "Let 'er rip."

He looked at me in surprise. "Really?" I had never let him touch the throttles before.

"Go ahead," I said. "Take her to almost full speed, but keep the port throttle a touch behind the others."

He nudged the levers gingerly at first, keeping the two right ones level with each other and the left slightly behind; then pushed them firmly. The three Libertys let out a surging roar, *Daisy* lifted her bow and started smacking over the waves instead of cutting through them, the wind blew through the opened wheelhouse windows with the force of a half-gale, the nearer waves blurred with speed—and we were flying, going fast as a mean thought, Young Sam laughing with delight like a kid half his age.

And in less than ten minutes the black launch was gone.

The dock in Port Jefferson harbor was where fishermen unloaded their catch—grungy enough that the *Daisy*, with her elegant lines and glistening varnish, stuck out among the scarred draggers and purse-seine boats like a Kentucky thoroughbred in a herd of plough-horses. The local trawlermen looked us over with amusement, asked us if we were lost, and made jokes about bottle-fishing. But Young Sam said the dock fit the description he'd been given. And the real reason for choosing a dock over our usual mooring became apparent when, just after dusk, a man in a pink suit and straw boater approached the *Daisy* bearing a large wicker hamper.

"I told you I was going to make this run, old sport," Gatsby exclaimed as he strode into the wheelhouse. He slapped me companionably where I was double-checking course and time to our rendezvous point, swept away my pencils and rulers, rolled up my chart and laid out the hamper's contents on my chart table: ham and cheese sandwiches, chicken salad, several bottles of beer, a bottle of champagne with glasses to match. "We're going to do this in style, like Cody would have done," he said. "By God but it's good to be on a real boat again!"

He went out on deck and paced from bow to stern, an admiral inspecting his flagship, then returned to the wheelhouse. Marcus and Young Sam had come up from the after cabin when they heard voices and at Gatsby's urging (the blinis having long ago been eaten) each took a sandwich and a beer.

I watched Gatsby as he opened the champagne and poured for everyone but him. I was annoyed at the man for sweeping away my instruments in such cavalier fashion yet charmed, as usual, by his enthusiasm, his forty-acre grin; his air of treating all restraints as lacy, temporary.

Tonight all those characteristics I had come to associate with him, and in particular that charge of surplus energy, had swelled yet again; doubled if not tripled in power, overflowing the small wheel-house. In the calmest of circumstances he was never still but on this night his restlessness was so exaggerated—he kept thumping my shoulder and back, pounding his own thigh, drumming fingers, adjusting his hat, taking it off to smooth his hair, sitting, stand-ing up, over and over again—that it cried out, loud and clear, for something besides a smuggling run or day-to-day concerns being responsible for such manic levels of activity. Of course I knew, now, where the extra energy came from, but the smile and charm seemed so out of proportion to their audience that, paradoxically, they had the opposite effect from what presumably was intended: making us realize they were not really directed at Jon Laine or his crew, but rather were Gatsby's instruments, the tools he used on everyone to achieve the goals he'd set. And I remembered Jordan's words about con artists, and felt disloyal.

Two hours later he still had not settled down. I'd piloted us out of Port Jefferson and, proceeding at a quarter speed, we were maybe ten minutes from rendezvous with the *Loch Alsh*. It was an average night for a late-summer run: wind ten to fifteen knots from the south-southwest, scudding cirrus that by hiding then revealing a gibbous moon just over the eastern horizon imparted a feeling of theatre to the scene—a great drape of darkness dropping then lifting to reveal waves that were always different, part of the sea's ceaseless melodrama.

The wash of wake, the grumble of Libertys filled our ears. Marcus and Young Sam stood on either side of the wheelhouse, keeping lookout. Gatsby had wanted to steer and he did so as competently as he did everything else, holding the wheel like a swordsman his épée, keeping steady on our course of north by east.

"This is my first run and also my last," he told me. The red light illuminating our compass made his handsome features appear almost demonic. "Daisy and I are leaving together, leaving America, I think we'll go to the Continent, it's all set. She's telling her husband tomorrow."

I was only half listening. I felt more nervous than usual about this run. I figured this was because it had been so long since we rendezvous-ed in this area. The nature of Long Island Sound, so caged compared to the open Atlantic—along with the occasional glare of moonlight and the reappearance of that black launch yesterday—had destroyed the routine feel that characterized our last trip into the Sound. At least we could be reasonably certain that no cutters would interrupt the loading here, since our Coast Guard contact was still on payroll ... but Gatsby's mind was on higher things.

"She's everything I remembered, from Louisville; like someone from a different planet, Jon, delicate and beautiful. A place where it's always spring, the kind of spring they have there with jasmine flowers, and croquet on the lawns, and the old, old families ..."

We were close to the rendezvous point now and I opened the door to warn Marcus. Though Gatsby was still talking I no longer heard his words. His tone now felt a little different from earlier: I sensed he was talking as much to charm himself, to convince himself, as to charm and convince others. Then Young Sam knocked on the portside window and pointed. After a few seconds I saw it too, a blot on the stain of darkness, a ship about the size of the *Loch Alsh*—you could never tell for sure at sea, at night, but this was the right time and the right place. I flicked our searchlight on and off, but the ship did not respond.

Then a green lamp on the dark shape flashed the required code, and I flashed back. I leaned out the door and called, "Get ready with lines and bumpers."

As we drew near the familiar bulk of the *Loch Alsh*, its rust-and-weed-covered steel lifting then subsiding by *Daisy*'s starboard side, I felt my nervousness recede. Gatsby had asked to handle the raft-up and I stood outside the wheelhouse to supervise, though this was hardly necessary given Gatsby's skill. Young Sam was a competent deckhand by now, and as Gatsby eased us alongside, Sam and Marcus neatly threw lines aboard the freighter. Dark shapes leaned over the ship's side to watch. Someone fumbled the line up forward and Marcus heaved it up again, with the same result. I yelled to the men above, "Can you pick up forward?" and someone shouted down, "Hold your horses, will ya?"

It was not a Scotsman—the accent was pure American, or Canadian I supposed. They must have brought new crew aboard in Newfoundland.

"How many cases we got this time?" I called.

"What?"

The forward line went taut as the freighter's crew at last secured our bow.

"How many extra cases?"

"Nothin' extra," came the reply. It was a higher voice than the previous one, and it too lacked the rasping "r"s of a Scottish accent. I was curious now, I'd heard nothing about a crew change on the *Loch Alsh*; the last time we took a load off her, south of Fire Island, the accents were all Scottish. I stuck my head back in the wheelhouse. "Jay," I said, "did they switch crew on the *Loch Alsh*?"

He stared at me. Clearly he'd been thinking of something completely different from the technicalities of smuggling. I didn't have to guess what it was.

"The crew," I said impatiently, "on the ship—are they same as always? No change?"

Finally he nodded. I looked up at the freighter again. Two men had propped the Jacob's ladder on the gunwale and were getting ready to unroll it. Before, they'd always had the ladder down and ready. Before, they'd handled the lines professionally. My heart rate was speeding up. There had to be an explanation; the *Loch Alsh* had flashed the required code, and only Wolfshiem's men knew that.

"I need to talk to Captain Murray," I called.

A pause.

"He's in the engine room. What do you want?"

"Get him. I'll wait."

The ladder unfurled suddenly, its lower rungs bouncing off our gunwale, splashing in the inky water between the two hulls. "We're sendin' somebody down," the higher voice said.

"I need to—"

A man sat on the ship's railing, getting ready to swing on to the ladder. Another climbed to the rail beside him. In a fast pulse of panic nothing seemed right to me tonight and I called to Young Sam and Marcus, "Drop the lines!"

"What?" Marcus said.

"Drop the lines. *Now!*"

"They're our lines," Young Sam objected.

"We'll pick 'em up later. *Do* it."

I think they heard the tension in my voice. Young Sam ran aft, Marcus forward. One of the freighter's men was already climbing down. I hopped back into the wheelhouse. Young Sam was hidden by the after deckhouse but Marcus was straightening, the bow-line gone. From aft I heard the boy shout, "Okay!"

"Hold on!" I cried. Gatsby was still at the helm—I shouldered him aside, turned the wheel left, and gunned all three throttles. Gatsby staggered backwards. The engines let out a howl, *Daisy* lifted her bow and canted hard to port as we veered away from the freighter's hull. A champagne glass slid off the chart table and smashed on the deck.

"What're you *doing?*" Gatsby yelled.

"Just making sure," I yelled back, peering behind us; the *Loch Alsh* looked as black and silent as it usually did. I would be ridiculed, I thought, for being a nervous Nellie.

A yellow-orange flash lit up the freighter's bridge-wing. And another. I heard two pops.

From behind the ship's hull a smaller shape appeared, black too, with a growing dash of pale foam at its bow to indicate it was gaining speed. I sensed as much as saw the round shape of the craft's pilothouse.

Now another series of flashes lit the *Loch Alsh*'s bridge wing. Something banged into our cabin, I wasn't sure where. And again. An aft window in the cabin shattered. I heard, above the wind, the woodpecker rhythm of automatic fire.

Gatsby had been staring through the aft windows. Abruptly, he disappeared into the cabin.

I pushed the throttles to near full speed, hoping Marcus and Young Sam were holding tight. The Libertys made their leopard sound. *Daisy* lifted her bow yet higher, then settled into wave-slapping mode. I hung on to the wheel, struggling to gain control of my thoughts. The *Loch Alsh* had been hijacked, that much was clear. The hijackers' boat was on our tail. Certainly the *Daisy* was faster, but we would be within range of the launch for minutes yet. I twisted the wheel to one side, then the other, canting *Daisy* to port then starboard, hoping to evade the bullets.

Gatsby climbed back up the companionway. The compass light reflected on a shiny bulk of metal in his arms: the Colt-Browning. He opened the portside door, bracing himself against the jamb, held the machine-gun at waist level, and aimed aft.

"Turn to port!" he yelled, and I did so.

The machine-gun roared. Its sound was vast, brutal, exhilarating. For the length of the burst it stuffed my eardrums with explosions, eight per second, and made me joyous: glad we were fighting back—happy because for once we were not helpless against the might of whatever sons of bitches wished to steal my boat and most likely kill us all into the bargain.

The dark behind us flared twice, three times with return fire. Gatsby let off two more bursts.

These were not returned. I straightened our course southward, away from the *Loch Alsh*.

After three or four minutes Gatsby came back inside and with a grunt of effort laid the machine-gun carefully at the chart table's base. Smoke curling from the barrel filled the wheelhouse with the crisp fumes of battle. He was grinning.

"Haven't had so much fun since the war," he said cheerfully. "Did I ever tell you, old sport, I was a major in a Lewis-gun detachment?"

I shook my head, peering alternately into the darkness ahead of us, then at the compass. We were heading southwest now, still more than three miles from Long Island's shore. I figured we had put enough distance between us and the launch to slow down and check for damage. I pulled the throttles back to a quarter speed and asked Gatsby to steer again. I leaned out the door and yelled, "Marcus? Young Sam? Everyone okay?"

"What the hell's goin' on?" Marcus yelled back—he was still up forward, hanging on against the surge and bump of our run.

"Rum pirates," I called back. "They must have hijacked the ship … Young Sam?"

It was hard to hear against the slam of waves and the engines' rumble, but what I heard back was nothing.

"Sam!" I yelled again.

Marcus started aft. I told Gatsby to keep heading southwest, then followed. I didn't see Young Sam for a minute—he wasn't where he should have been, by the starboard cleats—but something else, in this night of off-things, was different: and that was a dark slump blurring the angle between deck and transom.

Marcus kneeled, rolled it toward him, and I saw the pallor of Young Sam's face as he looked up at Marcus and said something I couldn't hear.

Chapter Fourteen

"Don't talk," Marcus told Young Sam. "Lemme see."

I kneeled by the boy's head. His shirt was shiny and dark; when Marcus opened it, the pale stomach inside held a patch of a similar glint. Sam groaned—and I was back on Garfield Avenue, where the air had been cold not hot, and the ground did not rock back and forth, but the mouth and eyes were open in agony and there was nothing I could do for Seppo.

Young Sam groaned again.

"He's hit in the stomach," Marcus said. "Left side. We need to get him to a doctor quick."

I was still staring at Young Sam's belly. The shine seemed to move. He was bleeding heavily. At least that meant he was alive, his heart was pumping. This was not Seppo, this was Young Sam, and he was still alive.

"Jon!" Marcus shouted, and shook my shoulder.

"All right," I replied.

"I need bandages," Marcus said. "*Now!*"

I looked behind us but amid the black and teeming waters saw no sign of the launch. I went back to the wheelhouse. Broken glass crunched under my shoes. I grabbed a handful of linen napkins from the picnic hamper, took them as quickly as I could to Marcus, ran back to the wheelhouse.

"Young Sam's been hit," I told Gatsby, and nudged the throttles to half speed. Now I had to shout against the engines' noise. "We have to get to the trucks fast, get him to a doctor."

Gatsby turned to look at me; I could see only the half of his face, tinted pink as his suit by the compass light.

"We can't go there," he said, half shouting too. "If the hijackers know about the *Loch Alsh*, they could know about the dock."

I had changed our course to south by west for Port Jefferson, I did not change it back.

"Then we'll go to that fish pier in Port Jefferson, an'—"

"Too public. We'll take him to the boathouse."

"Too long."

"We can call from there—"

"It'll take too long!"

"This boat can go—"

"Damn it, he's bleeding from the stomach!" I almost screamed it. "I'm not risking his life jiss so you can—so you can keep everything *hidden*!"

The rage and devastation scorched me inside. I think Gatsby noticed them. He was silent for a half minute then said, "All right, we'll go to my dock, in West Egg. It's maybe an extra ten, fifteen minutes at top speed—right? But at least we know there's a 'phone. And from my house we can take him right away, in one of the cars."

Marcus showed up then. "More bandages?" he said. Gatsby handed him napkins. I switched on the chart light and plotted a course for the Eggs. Navigating, steering, keeping lookout for the gas buoy off East Egg Point allowed my mind to slouch back from the brink of panic.

Once past the buoy I reduced speed. Gatsby began giving directions in his calm voice and within three or four minutes I spotted the green light marking the dock across the inlet from his château.

"Is that where we tie up?" I asked, pointing at the light.

"No." Gatsby's voice now took on a tone so glowing and rich I could only read it as pleasure. "That's *East* Egg. The Buchanans' dock. It's why—" He didn't go on, but pointed away from the light, to that dock off the beach where I'd gone swimming after his last party. It seemed like a year ago. "Tie up there."

I aimed *Daisy* along the dark outline of Gatsby's dock. The tide was near low and we bumped shallows going in but managed to scrape close enough. Gatsby climbed to the dock and disappeared. I assumed he had gone to the telephone, to get help. I tied us with a breast-line to a piling, cut the engines and went aft. Marcus was sitting next to Young Sam, his right hand pressing napkins to the boy's stomach.

"How is he?" I asked.

"Where are we?"

"Gatsby's house. West Egg. He's gone for help, I think."

"You *think?*"

But he had. A few minutes later Gatsby showed up on the dock with a clutch of men. He gave orders in the same calm voice, and I remembered what he'd said about his war experience. Three of the men hopped down to *Daisy's* deck and gathered around Young Sam. They unfolded a blanket and lifted the boy onto it; I heard Young Sam cry out in pain as they did so. With our help they lifted the boy high to place him on the dock, then climbed after him.

"Put him in the station wagon," Gatsby ordered. "Easy now."

Young Sam didn't yelp this time as they picked him up and set off for the house. I started to follow. "Where are you going?" Gatsby called.

I turned. "I'm going with him."

"No you're not."

"What do you mean?"

He gestured at *Daisy*. "Someone has to bring the boat back."

"That can wait."

"It's not a request," Gatsby replied in the same sure voice. A staff officer's voice, I thought, a voice used to being obeyed without question. He was still worried about publicity—if the cops investigated the shooting, if the *Daisy* was found at his dock with bullet holes in her wheelhouse—I realized, all of a sudden, that I didn't give a damn about any of it.

"I'm not leaving him," I said. "You can get someone else to move the boat."

He didn't respond for a beat or two, and in those seconds I turned and started for the house. I expected him to shout after me: a major berating a lieutenant, a boss scolding a worker, a rich man summoning his servant. I think, despite my preoccupation with Young Sam, I felt something for him then; without formulating . it in the front of my mind, I was conscious in back of how much harder it was to fake these things—staff officer, aesthete, lord of the manor—than to be born into their ease as Tom Buchanan had been. I believe I heard him say, softly, "All right, all right," and that's how I want to remember him: as someone who at game's end chose friendship, however reluctantly, over advantage.

I did not hurry at first, expecting some further compromise or offer. The night around me remained silent but for the shushing of wavelets, the ratchet of frogs, the slip of my feet on the lawns and the scrape of breath in my throat as I walked more quickly, then trotted, then ran as fast as I could after Young Sam.

—

He lasted the whole way. We laid Young Sam in back of the same yellow station wagon that had ferried me to the first of Gatsby's parties. Marcus crouched beside him. He had used up the last of the napkins to stanch the wound in the boy's gut. I sat in the next seat, cutting up our jackets with my deck-knife to use as bandages.

The driver was not the chauffeur I'd known but one of Wolfshiem's crew, a squat man who said almost nothing and drove fast around curves. This was fine given the circumstances but it made Young Sam moan again as his body shifted, so eventually I climbed over my seat, kneeled next to Marcus, wormed one hand carefully under Young Sam's back and held his shoulders as best I could against the swerves. When I asked the driver where we were going he said simply, "Nassau Hospital." When I asked him if there wasn't a doctor closer by he only grunted.

After awhile I realized the boy was no longer moaning. His face was a round blur in the dark. In the sweep of headlamps from a car coming the other way I saw his eyes were closed. I saw, also, the pimples across his cheeks, and this sign of youth caused my chest to seize. "Don't give up, Young Sam," I croaked at him, "don't give up!"

"He's going," Marcus said. "Where is that fucking hospital. Where is the hospital?" he yelled at the driver. "The hospital!"

"Almost there," the driver said.

"There's too much blood," Marcus shouted, "too much!"

"Don't give up, please don't give up" was all I could think of to say, and I kept repeating it as if in prayer, though it wasn't: as a former member of the Finnish Socialists I did not believe in bourgeois religion, but maybe—my thoughts scattering like prairie chickens in all directions as they tried to avoid what might be happening in the circle of my arms—maybe that's all prayer really was, a repetition, a rhythm, a way to inscribe some kind of order on the screaming chaos of events such as this …

The station wagon braked to a halt outside the white portico of a mansion somewhat smaller than Gatsby's. A couple of minutes later, summoned by the driver, a group of men and women in white gently pulled Young Sam from our arms and placed him on a stretcher. "Please don't give up," I said, though he couldn't hear me, and I kept saying it even as the white-clad people gathered around the stretcher, lifted it, and carried Young Sam inside.

—

I was still repeating "Please don't give up" two hours later. It was almost an hour after one of the men in white came out and said quietly, "I'm sorry, but—"

I didn't listen to anything after that. I think I had known he would die from the start; part of my brain, however, would not slam that bolt home. Marcus sat with me for a while, his arm around my shoulders when others weren't looking. Eventually he got sick of my mindless repetition, my refusal to accept what had happened, the tears that slimed out at regular intervals, the wretched coughs that followed the sobs, and left me alone.

Finally I got tired of it too and just sat on a bench in the down-stairs hallway of Nassau Hospital, smoking and waiting. I knew there was going to be trouble; you could not show up at a hospital with a boy dying from a bullet in the gut without the cops getting involved. But I did not know what to do next, and didn't care. Anyway the hospital was busy, I learned later there had been a bad car crash in Huntington. The next person to talk to me was not a cop.

"Jon," she said. "Jon!"

I looked up. Stella Wolfshiem was half-kneeling in front of me. She had been crying, too. Her face was puffed, her mascara had run and her eyes were pink. I remembered then, Young Sam was her cousin.

"Please don't give up," I said, it seemed that was all I knew how to say. From a room nearby I heard a woman wailing, a man shout-ing, someone else interrupting. She reached out a hand and took one of mine.

"Jon."

She was crying now. As if to mimic her, my own tears flowed once more. I cleared my throat, started to cough again.

"I'm sorry," I grunted after the coughing stopped. Apparently I had regained my powers of original speech. I wiped my eyes with a sleeve. "I'm so sorry, Stella …"

"Marcus Fayerweather told me," she said and squeezed my hand hard. "I don't know what else you could have done. But you got to go now, Meyer says. The police will be here soon."

I realized vaguely that Gatsby must have got in touch with Wolfshiem; Stella was not here solely as a family member. I made no move to get up.

"Jon," she said again, and tugged at my hand. "I will explain things to them, but you've got to *leave*. I asked the nurse to call a taxi."

I stared at her. Despite her pink eyes and puffy face she was still one of the most beautiful women I had ever seen. And it didn't matter. I didn't care about pretty women anymore. I did not care

about rum-running, or money, or Gatsby. Nothing mattered compared to the body-memory of the boy lying in my arms as his breath
shallowed, as life drained out of him. Stella glanced behind her
now. New voices in some other room. The unseen woman wailed
still, as my mother had, as all women did the world over after their
men killed each other.

"Come on," she insisted, pulling at my arm now, "why don't you
come? I know you were friends, Sam would want you to."

I let her pull. Why couldn't she understand? My body would
have been happy to get up, to do what she asked; it was my mind
that did not have one percent of the strength required to do so. I
needed to explain this to her.

"Not just Young Sam," I said.

There'd been Seppo, lying dead in Garfield Avenue. He was
my friend too, a much closer friend than Young Sam had been, and
I had grieved for him. But the one I truly mourned, even when I
mourned Seppo, even as I cried for Young Sam, had always been
someone else. For the first time, I think, I wanted to stop lying
about it, to Stella but mostly to myself.

"Eiki," I said. "Stella—

'Yes?"

"See—I killed him, too."

She stopped tugging at my arm. She was looking at me as if all
of her wanted to understand and help; it seemed to me something
that women, not men, were truly capable of, and it made me love
them more. But even this was unimportant; the only part that really
mattered now was that someone else should finally know about my
brother.

—

I had come back from the Navy a week before Christmas in 1918.
We'd heard rumors of an influenza epidemic killing soldiers in
Europe, and that it might have spread to the Midwest. I found out
later—most of the news about it was stifled by wartime censors—the

Spanish 'flu had actually started in the Midwest before sneaking its way, in the bloodstreams of conscripts, to army camps in Europe.

But I was young and strong and figured it would not touch me. Even when I contracted a slight cough and fever on the train ride from Norfolk they dissipated soon enough and I paid them little heed. After all, I had spent a year in the Mediterranean, participated in the second battle of Durazzo, and been made an officer, albeit a junior one. Finland was days away from independence from Russia, and no mere cough would prevent me from raising a glass of brandy with my father to celebrate once I got home. I was keen to see my mother; most of all I longed to see Eiki, four years my junior but ever my closest friend and ally in the wars of growing up.

I still had the influenza, however, and I brought it home. My parents developed a fever. They got sick enough to send for a doctor, but we had little money, the medic was overwhelmed, and the combination meant he never showed up.

In the depths of our parents' illness my brother got sick too. From the very first his symptoms were more severe than theirs. His lungs filled overnight, and by the third day his face was the color of new ice and he was coughing up blood and mucus. My parents' health was now improving but they were very weak and could only watch, frail and stunned, as their younger son faded toward death.

And then he got better. For a day. I thought it was my care; I had made him soup, and tea, and held him as he drank; slept beside him at night. He had big eyes and bigger loyalty and when he looked at you in gratitude you would move the fireplace for him. Color returned to his cheeks and joy returned to that little house as his fever fell. He sat up in bed to eat. He called me "Lieutenant" and pretended to salute, and smiled when I brought him more soup.

Late that night the fever returned, his cough racked him, the blood from lungs and nose was more copious. I lay in bed holding him as he grew delirious, and his face turned blue again, and his breathing grew short and ragged; as at last, after one long, deep exhalation, he ceased breathing altogether.

There had been the world before in which Eiki, in ways we'd never recognized, was the turntable of our family; no matter what misfortunes befell us my kid brother would spin them around with a grin and a quip—even with one of his sulks, which we all understood were the midnight side of his good nature—and through him we always found another direction, another track on which to run, some form of happiness.

Now he was gone. Joy seemed something unimaginable, a different galaxy, a time before. Though the 'flu struck others nearby—the Winikainens next-door lost their daughter, Miina, with whom I had grown up—my parents, and especially my mother, never forgave me for bringing the disease home, for causing Eiki's death.

We didn't talk about Eiki; we tried our best not to think about him. All Scandinavians are good at chaining down their emotions and Finns, as I've implied before, are masters of the art. The spirit of *sisu*, of enduring without complaint, was strong in us, but of course that didn't work deep down, not in the secret chambers of the heart, not in the long run. Eventually my father asked me to leave their house. It was then I moved to Finn Town.

I did not tell Stella the details. Mostly I talked of the physical memory of holding Eiki as he died, as I had held Young Sam. I have spoken before of my belief in stories, as people's way of understanding one another; I was aware, however, that this did not always work in practice.

But Stella got it. I saw it in her face, and in her hands which now gripped both of mine with a strength that surprised me; in those late-night eyes that even in my broken state I could see held no half-shades of doubt or pretense.

"You didn't know," she said. "That wasn't your fault, either."

"It doesn't matter. Nothing had value after that. I know it sounds like I'm fishing for pity, but I used to believe in stuff, ah—"

I could not find the words, and had not the strength to try.

"*Baruch dayan emet*," she said then.

I looked at her.

"It's Hebrew. It means, 'Blessed is the one true judge'."

I shrugged.

"What it really means is you can't know everything, you're not God who controls everything."

"It don't work for me. I don't believe."

Now Stella shrugged. "That doesn't matter. It's more like saying, I am not responsible for things, I can't always help what happens, there's bigger stuff that runs our lives."

"I used to believe the opposite. I used to think, you have to help—" I stopped.

"*Baruch dayan emet*," Stella repeated. Her eyes burned into mine. "Say it."

I shook my head.

"*Say* it."

Those eyes.

"*Baruch dayan emet*," I said, twisting the vowels.

"Repeat it."

"*Baruch dayan emet.*"

We sat there silent for a while. Five minutes later a white-bearded man in a wide-brimmed black hat blundered through the hallway and Stella stood to greet him, to show him to the room from which the woman's wails had never stopped emerging. And right afterwards two cops showed up, Mineola town police, a sergeant and a constable. Stella intercepted them as they made their way toward me.

"He's still in shock," she told them. "He was Samuel's friend, they were just walking along East Cove Road and then there were men in cars, shooting"—she was looking at me sideways, to see if I took the hint—"bootleggers, probably—"

"Why don't you let him tell us," the sergeant said firmly. "Ralph? Take notes."

"She knows the whole story," I muttered, looking at the constable, who was gazing lustfully at Stella.

"We wanna hear it from you," the sergeant said. He was tall, stout, stooped, and had a crooked nose. The brim of his hat was

higher on one side. He half-squatted to look me in the face. I stared
back. Ever since my days in the union I have not trusted cops. The
dislike meshed easily with my sense of having nothing to lose, what
I thought of as my Eiki feeling, which now held a Young Sam over-
lay; nothing was of much import now.

"It's like she said," I told him finally. "We were just walking—"

"Where."

"Egg Landing," Stella said quickly. "They were looking for a
job—"

"Will ya *please* let him tell it?" the sergeant said. The constable
forced his eyes away from Stella.

"Yeah," I said. "We, uh, heard there was a job, there's all these
rich people there. We were just walking …"

With the occasional prompt from Stella I made up a story. Sam
and I worked at a garage, we needed extra money, we were walking
from one mansion to the next, one squad of bootleggers must have
been waiting to ambush another, we got trapped in the crossfire.
I said my piece without emotion or emphasis because of my Eiki
state: because with Eiki in my head I didn't give a tinker's damn
whether they believed me or not, maybe I even wanted them to
disbelieve me, for them to punish me somehow. Curiously, it was
my indifference that seemed to convince them.

So, I assumed, did the fold of green Stella handed the sergeant
along with a scrap of paper on which she had written Young Sam's
home address.

In the midst of all this, a couple of men started arguing loud
enough to drown out the woman, who was now only wailing in-
termittently. A door in the hallway opened and the white-bearded
man came out, still shouting at another fellow. The sergeant got
involved. The bearded man was a rabbi and he wanted Young Sam's
body released for burial. The other man said it must be held for an
autopsy. Stella tried to mediate. Everyone ignored her.

I left them there. For the first time in hours I got to my feet. I
looked around for Marcus. I found out later that Wolfshiem's driver
had left as soon as Young Sam was admitted and Marcus, assuming

a black man would automatically attract the suspicion of white cops, had gone with him. He had told me once that rum-running didn't feel much different for his people; they were always smuggling themselves into and out of white America.

I traversed the hallway and a lobby. A nurse asked me where I was going; I ignored her. I walked to the portico, down the steps, outside.

It was cooler in the open. In front of the hospital was a wide lawn. I wondered if every big house on Long Island had a lawn. This one smelled of clover and sky.

"*Baruch dayan emet,*" I whispered as I walked. It did not mean anything to me. Bigger forces made things happen and sometimes people tried to stop them: it seldom if ever worked. This was not new and it did not change or palliate the pain these forces caused.

But Stella had told me to repeat those words. I remembered what I'd thought about repetition when I was mumbling "Don't give up" to Young Sam. "Don't give up" hadn't worked for Young Sam or for Eiki. "*Baruch dayan emet*" held no more power. But Stella had told me to repeat it, and tonight I would go along with what Stella said.

Chapter Fifteen

By noon the next day I was back at Mike's, drinking coffee, smoking; staring into space while Mike banged dishes and muttered "*gamoto*." He'd been cursing and banging pots ever since I told him about Young Sam.

The mood in Mike's was bleak. No one cranked my phonograph, no one even played poker. I was coughing from the cigarettes, of course, and from being back in the smoky environment of the Land of Ashes but also from fatigue. The hospital had called me a taxi at 5 a.m. and by 7 I was back in my room but had not been able to sleep. I had neither interest nor the energy to do what I should have done, which was return to West Egg to pick up *Daisy*.

Eventually, around 9, I had dragged my knackered bones to Mike's.

At 11 Marcus showed up. His face was hollow and he wore no hat. He drank two coffees without saying a word then walked to the garage to telephone Essie-Mae, which was what he always did when he felt low.

I was in the same place and doing the same things at noon as I had been doing at 9 when George Wilson stomped in. I had told him about Young Sam on my way past the garage but he looked at me as if he couldn't understand what I said, though he must have since he muttered "That's too bad" in a tone like saying "What did you expect." I felt anger then and almost snapped back. His features were blank and unhappy, which was normal; he looked sick, which was how he'd looked for the last two or three weeks, but today he was worse. His eyes were sunk in lilac hollows, his skin so pale it was green. I thought, he had not known Young Sam well, and tried to forgive his indifference.

Now, as Wilson entered the coffeeshop the blankness had left his face; he had the same narrowed eyes and taut posture as when he'd leveled a gun at me. He stood by the cash register and stared at Mike.

"Just wanna tell ya," he hissed, "I got proof this time. Someone's running around with her. I got *proof*," he repeated.

Mike had his eyes on Wilson's hands, but they held no gun. Everyone in the coffeeshop—myself and Stavros and a walk-in customer, as well as Mike—stared at Wilson. Now I understood the real reason Wilson had not reacted when I told him about Young Sam; there was no room for anything in his head that did not concern his wife and what she was doing to him. I thought of Mike's words about the jealousy of gods and for a second, even through my sadness and my guilt, I almost admired Wilson: to love someone so hard, so obsessively that you could not feel any other emotion seemed, on that particular afternoon, a quality to be both pitied and desired.

"Jiss so you know, I'm taking her away now. She's done goin' out on her own—"

"You lock her up?" Mike interrupted. His hands wiped each other strongly in his apron.

"I tole you," George Wilson announced, looking around at all of us. "We're goin' out West. Whether she wants to or not…. You'll never see her again."

"So you make this car deal," Mike said, after a pause.

"No. We're going anyway—once I get my pay. You'll never see her again," he repeated, and stomped out. Stavros made a comment in Greek and Mike replied in their language. My stomach was growling but the thought of eating made me feel sick. I wanted a drink, yet had no desire for liquor.

Young Sam's features, pale and blurred, kept floating to the forefront of my brain; and of course, every time, they turned into the image I had tried for so long to forget, of Eiki's face in the insufficient harbor of my arms, his face in the circle of our family in that daguerreotype; and my tears swelled like water from marshland that had soaked up too much rain.

I wondered how I'd ever thought I could hold that memory down for any length of time; I remembered Eiki as freshly as if he had died last week. Time seemed to have no meaning or measure when it came to remembering people you loved. I supposed this was true of Gatsby and his memories of Daisy when he courted her in Louisville ...

The hours warped and shifted. Even on this strange baked afternoon they seemed to stretch—though I had the feeling it wasn't much later that Gatsby's cream-yellow phaeton rolled to a stop in front of Wilson's gas pump.

It was hotter than yesterday. Heat from the roadway made the car's chrome shimmer in the air between. The Rolls-Royce held two passengers and a driver; it was facing the creek, away from Mike's, so I did not recognize them at first.

Wilson appeared at the doorway to his shop. He leaned on the jamb, watching the Rolls. The driver got out and walked toward him—not Gatsby, as I'd automatically assumed, but Tom Buchanan. I watched in mild curiosity, wondering if Wilson's "proof" had finally implicated Buchanan, but they seemed to be talking normally.

Now two passengers got out: a man in white flannels, who held the car door for a woman with bobbed, bleached-gold hair under a small straw bonnet—someone who leaned backwards as she stretched. It was Jordan Baker. The man, I now saw, was Nick Carraway.

Finally Wilson nodded. He walked to the gravity pump, dragged a nozzle to the phaeton's fuel pipe, and stood there motionless as he filled the tank.

A few minutes later the Rolls and its occupants were gone. Jordan had never even glanced at the coffeeshop to see if I was there. I told myself I didn't care, and mostly I did not. A cloud of ash and dust summoned by the phaeton's wheels rose, was sheepdogged by a lazy breeze to join the greater smoke from the Land of Ashes. Myrtle Wilson, her hair unkempt, emerged from the garage and stood with hands on hips, staring after the car. I felt a reluctant empathy for her: we were two people who had just been ignored by our lovers, or ex-lovers—treated like we no longer existed. The pale, hooded eyes of Dr. T.J. Eckleburg watched over the scene with their usual vast indifference.

Now Wilson returned to the coffeeshop. I saw Mike glance toward the storeroom where he kept his shotgun, but Wilson's mood had changed. He was not smiling, and he still looked ill, but he no longer glowered at Mike as if he wished to shoot him dead.

"Made that deal," he said, "just now."

"You buy *that* bus?" Mike asked incredulously.

"Rolls-Royce!" Stavros confirmed. "Wow."

"No," Wilson said, "that one's not his." I remembered how Gatsby had insisted on staying away from the garage operation; if Wilson did not know the Rolls belonged to one of his employers, his precautions must have worked.

"He'll let me have the *Ford*, for low money," Wilson continued. "I can sell it for twice that in town, maybe more." He looked around the coffeeshop. "Maybe more!" he repeated, and for what felt to me like the first time ever, a wire of excitement drew current through his voice.

"Now I don't have to wait to get paid," he continued. "So we'll be gone from here day after tomorrow. Latest. Day after *tomorrow!*" he crowed, and left, slamming the door so hard it shook the flimsy walls.

I lit another cigarette. My coffee cup was empty. I had smoked so much and drunk so much coffee this morning that my hands jittered when I lit the match. For the first time in my life I thought about quitting: quitting cigarettes, coffee, even booze. I really did not want to end up looking like George Wilson.

I still had no desire for a drink.

—

I was still sitting in that booth when the Rolls came back.

It was evening now, a little cooler. I'd left the diner only twice, to visit the outhouse. Mike insisted on frying me a plate of liver and onions, of which I ate three bites to keep him off my back. Halfway through the afternoon he went into the storeroom for a nap and left me on watch in case customers came in.

Alone in the little restaurant, I put Ethel Waters on the phonograph. She seemed to sing mostly about her man leaving, and the depth of loss in her voice, not to mention how the songs' rhythms flooded then disconnected, to flood and disconnect again, hooked into how I was feeling, which only made me feel sadder, but that was OK; I was done with hiding from grief. In a strange twist of emotion, of *Baruch dayan emet* perhaps, feeling sadder felt right or at least more so than hiding from what I knew I felt anyway, deep down. A couple of track workers came in looking for supper and I called for Mike.

Now a screaming came from the garage. Myrtle must have gotten out, despite George's surveillance. I heard the words "You dirty *coward*!" and an indistinct reply from her husband. Everyone at Mike's was looking out the coffeeshop's windows toward the garage as the phaeton reappeared.

The Rolls was coming from the direction of New York and moving fast. The breeze had shifted a little so there was marginally less smoke to obscure the western end of our poor street, and despite the failing light I spotted the automobile from a couple of hundred yards away.

So did Myrtle Wilson. She ran from the garage, her blue skirt flapping with the speed of her passage, waving both arms as the car drew level. Jordan was driving, I saw her milky-gold hair, hatless now, shine in the sun's late rays. I expected her to brake and come to a stop, as Tom had stopped for Myrtle when he drove us to Manhattan.

Instead, the car seemed to wobble, away at first: then, with all the sickening inevitability of accident, it swerved in the other direction—straight into Myrtle as she plunged into its path.

Even from my booth I heard the thud: hollow, loud. The grille and fender hit Myrtle Wilson and lifted her into the air, seven or eight feet high, her face upturned and arms and dress spread wide, as if she had finally learned how to fly.

Chapter Sixteen

The phaeton continued down the road, and did not slow; it left the usual devil of ashes in its wake.

Everything else that was capable of movement, it seemed, moved to help Myrtle Wilson now she no longer needed it. The two workmen, Mike and I left the coffeeshop at a run, though there'd been something in the quality of that "thud" which felt horribly final. Marcus emerged from the warehouse. A car coming from the direction of Long Island stopped near her body and disgorged two men. Another stranger showed up out of nowhere.

Myrtle lay on her back. Her head was bent to the left, one arm splayed, one hip crossed unnaturally over the other. Her eyes were open and her face held an expression, half amazed, half distant, as if flying had proved easier than she'd ever imagined. Blood dripped from her lips into the ash. Her blouse had been ripped halfway off her torso; her right breast hung bare over a wide, deep wound that seemed to smile beneath its curve. The nipple was half erect and the skin around it seemed white as paper compared to the surrounding flesh, the blue muslin below, all of which were soaked in a profligacy of blood.

Apart from her wounds, she did not look dead; in fact, she looked quite beautiful, but drained of the heat she once gave off—that source of heat from which we all, however casually, had drawn.

From a pocket in the torn dress, a magazine lay exposed.

Town Tattle.

Marcus kneeled beside her and felt Myrtle's throat. "Hey," one of the strangers said aggressively, "he shouldn't do that."

"He was a medic in the war, you *malaka*," Mike snarled at him. Marcus ignored them both; he kept kneeling by Myrtle's body, his thumb pressed against the side of her throat, for at least two minutes. Finally he shook his head. I felt sorry for him—it was the second time in as many days that he'd watched someone die. "Somebody should call an ambulance," he said hoarsely, getting to his feet and looking down at Myrtle, "but it's too late for her."

"They never even stopped," one of the strangers complained, looking east to where the Rolls had disappeared into the stretching shadows of dusk. "They never even slowed down!"

Somebody should tell George, I thought, and turned to look at the garage; but he was already there, moving like a sleepwalker from the garage door, eyes popping out of dark sockets, both hands (one still clutching a rag) pressed over his mouth as if to stifle the weird sounds emerging from that orifice as he stared at the body in the center of our little group.

He never came much closer. The strangled sounds grew in volume to a yell whose meaning we could just make out: "Oh *goo*-awd! Oh *goo*-awd!" he screamed through the greasy rag, over and over and over, as Mike fetched blankets and we lifted her body onto them and then lifted it again by the blanket's corners.

A peacock-blue Ford coming from the west swerved into the forecourt as we carried Myrtle inside the garage and laid her on a workbench. It was Buchanan's automobile, the one he had promised to George Wilson. More dust and ash rose around the car as it stopped. This was normal for our little neighborhood but today it felt more pervasive than usual; as if death, like the Bible said, elicited greater quantities of ashes and dust than even the wretched living could stir up in this foul place.

Buchanan emerged from the Ford, adjusting jacket and hat, and walked toward the garage with a "What's this all about" sort of stride. From the edge of my sight I saw he was followed by a woman with light-gold hair whom I took to be Daisy, since I'd last seen Jordan in the Rolls. But when I looked at her straight I saw it was Jordan: Jordan, and Nick Carraway. For a second or two my brain strove to catch up—I had last seen Buchanan driving these two in the Rolls Royce that hit Myrtle—had Tom somehow circled around, abandoned the phaeton, hopped into his own car with these passengers, and showed up now to allay suspicion? But my brain, it seemed, had not completely lost its sense of time, and the timing here was wrong.

And once Buchanan reached the edge of our group, and stopped, the jauntiness of his carriage seemed to drain from him. As he recognized Myrtle I saw his face muscles slacken. Then, abruptly and arrogantly, he shouldered his way through the onlookers to stand quite still over Myrtle's body: while Jordan and Carraway hung back, the flannel man holding her arm as if to support her, though he was the one who looked more frail; while a siren sounded outside and a cop dismounted from his motorcycle; as Wilson, who had retreated to the door of his little office, watched us with those bulging eyes, hands still covering his mouth, still screaming "Oh *goo*-awd! Oh *goo*-awd!" so loudly that it seemed to go against nature, it seemed even disrespectful to Myrtle—no one could think about her properly, nobody within range of that caterwauling could let in the quiet that marked and allowed for the passage of death.

I walked over to Wilson, gripped his shoulder, and shook him. "George," I said. "George!" He ignored me utterly, his eyes fixed as always on his wife. Tom Buchanan appeared beside me. His presence, oddly, did what I'd been unable to achieve by shaking him. Wilson stared at Tom Buchanan. "*You* don't have to tell me it was the phaeton," he said, his voice less high than when he screamed but just as stressed. "I *know* what kinda car!"

Buchanan stared at him. He glanced at the group surrounding his dead lover.

"The phaeton hit her? You mean, the yellow Rolls?"

Wilson's eyes were fixed, as if he was seeing the accident all over again, which perhaps he was. He nodded slowly.

Buchanan's mouth went thin. He gripped Wilson's other shoulder, and shook him harder than I had.

"That phaeton wasn't mine," he said. "D'you hear? I drove it earlier but it *wasn't mine!*"

Still Wilson stared at him, and now Buchanan shook him even more roughly, so that the mechanic's long frame seemed to dance.

"I told you," Buchanan repeated. "I drove it into town, gave it back to the owner this morning—haven't seen it all afternoon. I'm just bringing you that Ford we've been talking about—remember?"

"I *know* that car," Wilson insisted, loudly. The cop came over, followed by the flannel man.

"You knew that car?" the cop asked Wilson.

"I know that car," Wilson repeated.

"I'm a friend of his," Buchanan told the cop. "He says he knows the car that did it, it's a yellow phaeton, a Rolls Royce."

"And what color's your car?" the cop asked Buchanan, glancing at me—I suppose I was staring at both of them in turn as at a tennis match, trying for all my own shock to pick up tips on how to spin stories to the police.

"Mine's a blue car, a coupé," Buchanan said.

"We've come straight from New York," Carraway added helpfully.

"Yeah, he just drove up," someone offered—another stranger among the swelling group of voyeurs—"he was in that blue Ford." The cop lost interest, and turned away to question someone else.

—

I have had occasion to notice before how much more attention is paid to the impecunious dead, and even to those around, than was ever paid to them when they were alive. Whereas until today almost no one knew or cared to know George Wilson—indeed, had his garage been legitimate, it would have gone bankrupt for lack of custom a long time before—tonight, with the body of his dead wife laid out among the greasy wrenches and scraps of manifold, he and

Myrtle were never without company. More people appeared out-side, drawn by rumor to stare at the dregs of tragedy within. Four men—all unknown to me, except for the two who had run to help when she was hit—stayed with Wilson as he went back to his usual pursuit of screaming from the office doorway, then subsiding into sobs, before collapsing to a squat against the frame.

Buchanan had left after talking to the cop. Jordan and Carraway left with him. Oddly, after all the time I had once spent thinking about Jordan Baker, I had hardly realized she was there, and now I barely noticed she had gone.

I tried to help as well but found that I could not. That is, I could stay by Wilson, if such counted as comfort, but I did not know how to help beyond that. The grief that always lay inside me from Eiki—augmented by the different griefs from Seppo, and now Young Sam—seemed repelled, the way the positive poles of two magnets repelled each other, by the grief of Myrtle's husband.

Marcus made another call to Essie-Mae.

Finally an ambulance arrived and took Myrtle's body away. A slim young woman, gloriously drunk and wearing a long dress and many bracelets, staggered in fifteen minutes later, saw George, and fainted, to a musical tinkling from the bracelets. Someone said she was Myrtle's sister and someone else gave her a ride to the hospital from which the ambulance had come.

It still felt wrong to leave. I found a seat on the floor, my back against the wheel panel of, I think, a Pierce-Arrow. In my mind I kept hearing Myrtle's voice, saying "You don't live forever, right?" Out of sheer exhaustion I fell asleep.

I awoke to the sound of Mike setting a cup of coffee and a plate of toast on the office desk. The garage was dark but a wedge of watery light streamed from the open doorway. The garage faced southeast: it was dawn. Wilson was not in sight, though someone was mumbling behind me.

Blearily I looked around, and spotted him then, standing by a tiny window at the end of the garage. He was staring outside, maundering—pointing through the listless light.

I got up, joints a-crackle, and walked to the window. Mike limped after, frowning.

"He *murdered* her," Wilson was grunting. "You can fool me, but you can't fool God!"

I kept my expression neutral, vaguely sympathetic, though in my exhausted brain the only thought that came was, "Not again." Stella's god, Wilson's god—you called them when it was too late, when the injustices they had condoned all along reached their inevitable conclusion. What good was that? *"Baruch dayan emet"*— blessed is the one true judge.... But once more the remembered sound of Stella repeating those words calmed me a little.

"What are you saying, George?" Mike asked him.

Wilson was still pointing, high and outside. I edged around his large, sweat-stained body to see what he was indicating. "Gasoline Alley" cartoons tacked to its edges confused the window-frame: in one of them a mechanic, in a garage that looked a lot like this one, was saying to a man in black suit and glasses, "Doc, you poor sardine, shut off that engine! Don't you know better than to run it in a closed garage?"

But this was not the Wilson who giggled at the antics of Walt Wallet. He was peering far beyond the window. "*God* told me whose car it is," he announced hoarsely. "God sees everything!"

His arm, index finger stiff and trembling, aimed straight through the grimy glass, through the steadily brightening smoke, at the giant, hooded eyes of Doctor T.J. Eckleburg.

—

I should have figured it out sooner. My only excuse was, I was tired; tired, and cross-cut with the various sorrows—my own, Stella's, Wilson's—so that screaming, raving and mindless appeals to an indifferent deity seemed unworthy of further attention or thought.

Eventually Wilson sat down, and I climbed the stairs to my room. There I was pulled from unconsciousness hours later by a shaking that in my sleep I dreamed was Wilson roughing me up in revenge for all the shakes I had given him.

But it was Mike. He was leaning over my head. Though judging by what light reflected on the wall it was full day now, my room, which like the rest of the building's rooms held only one narrow window, was mostly shade. With his big eyebrows lowered even further than usual Mike resembled a dark angel, vengeful and angry. "It is God, God, he says! The eyes of God tell him."

Not you too, I thought.

"What are you talking about?"

"God!" Mike repeated. "What he is looking at—the eyes of Eckleburg doctor!"

"I know," I said, letting my head fall on the pillow again. "I was there, Mike."

"You don't understand it. The Eckleburg eyes, they are like what you say, what Miss Baker say—only this little bit open." He brought his face even closer to mine. I smelled onions on his breath. "Look," he said, and lowered his eyelids halfway. Bedroom eyes.

"Still don't get it," I said stupidly.

"There was this man like dat." Mike swiveled, sat heavily on the bed beside me. He set elbows on knees and held his chin up with one hand. The other held a newspaper. "He come here after Myrtle is dead. I don' think of it till now." He gestured with the newspaper. What I could see of the headline read "Two Dead ... Bootleg War."

"This fellow, he don't wear no coat ..."

I sat up then. I felt fear drool down my stomach, like an echo of the blood Young Sam had lost.

"... but he have eyes like Eckleburg, dis man," Mike continued. "And he fat, an' short too, like they say. An' he talk, talk—talk a long time to George."

"Where is he now?" I asked. "George."

"George is gone." Mike did not lift his head from his hand. "He is gone all day since early, and nobody know where he went."

—

We only learned what happened later, and that seemed right. The sequence of deaths and somber connections over those two days held the kind of mass that implied inevitability, the momentum of fate, a lack of options for human intervention—the eyes of God, as Wilson understood it.

We called Gatsby's house, of course, but by then everything was over. Wilson had found Gatsby in the pool. He had shot Jay dead, then shot himself.

We tried over the next few days to reconstruct events. That morning, Wilson had made his way east—on foot or train for part of the journey, since he'd long ago sold all his cars and not yet sold Buchanan's, and was broke as usual. They tracked him as far as Little Neck. It seemed clear someone had told him to look for the phaeton's owner in West Egg.

We never learned for sure if it was Mineo, the gangster with Eckleburg's eyes, who Mike saw talking to Wilson—telling him who owned the Rolls, pointing him in the direction of West Egg to make trouble; maybe hoping George would bump off a rival of the d'Aquila gang, leaving Mineo's hands clean. It could have been another garage owner who told him, or some inspiration of his grief-occluded brain: whatever his reason, and whatever the route, by two p.m. Wilson had made the connection, both accurate and faulty, that the car was Gatsby's and that Gatsby had killed his wife. And he found his way to the château.

I felt numb. Past a certain point it seemed the mind could not absorb more drama, or additional loss. With Marcus I sat on the steps in front of those poor, attached concrete buildings we called home—smoking, coughing, drinking the English Tea Mike brought out to us. The coffeeshop was busy: Myrtle's death had attracted the curious to the garage, and they stayed on for drinks or dinner.

I tried not to think of Young Sam clearing tables, or seeking to intervene when George threatened me with a gun.

Outside it was not quite so hot. Smoke blanched the daylight, evening blotted out the smoke. The drawbridge rose and fell, the trains passed, one sometimes hiding another, the locomotives making their own smoke. In the growing dark people silhouetted in the yellow-lit windows of outbound carriages seemed as distant and cold as ghosts, as shades of the not-yet-dead. The eyes of Dr. T.J. Eckleburg watched them until night erased the billboard from my view, and all that was left was trains.

Epilogue

Funerals of course, and wakes took place. George's and Myrtle's, in New Jersey, was a family affair and none of us were invited. In Brooklyn, Mike, Marcus and I attended a post-burial wake for Young Sam. It was part of a week-long event, a *shiva* in a hot and stuffy apartment, at which people in ripped black clothes greeted each other mostly in Hebrew or in a dialect of German, and chatted and told stories. They served blinis, coffee and sweet pastries. A couple of Young Sam's younger cousins played with tops in a corner.

While most of the adults looked down at the mouth, the stories seemed to comfort them—everyone except Young Sam's mother, who sat in a corner, trying to smile, looking as if not much was holding her up. She must have known I was the skipper of the boat on which her son had been shot, for when we were introduced she looked at me with stark hatred in her eyes. I had hoped to see Stella there but was told she'd left to arrange the next food delivery. With the eyes of Young Sam's mother drilling into me in exactly the way my mother's used to, I had no desire to wait.

Gatsby's funeral was a few days later. I went alone. It was the third time in ten days I had traveled to West Egg—the last time on Wolfshiem's orders, to pick up *Daisy* and run her back to the "gio … & Sons" boathouse. He had wanted me to make the run at night, and when Marcus and I got there, Gatsby's château was dark. So was the mansion across the bay. The green light on the Buchanans' dock was out.

The taxi driver was excited to take me to Gatsby's; the murder-suicide, it seemed, was the most fascinating event to occur in this area for years. He was the only one who knew the truth of what happened. Gatsby had been the leader of a ring of Bolshevik spies; when he started spending on festivities the money he'd been sent to bribe President Harding's cabinet with, he was executed on direct orders from Moscow. I let him ramble, not really listening, until he started inveighing against traitors to America, at which point I told him Gatsby was a friend of mine who had fought with the U.S. Army in France, and he should not spread lies about people he'd never met.

I walked the last half mile, wondering as I walked to what extent Gatsby and I had been friends and whether a passion such as his for a woman, for everything she represented—for the permanence that money brought, as Jordan claimed—shorted out the connections he'd made with everyone else. In the end we'd had very different ideas about what we thought important, and it had prevented us from ever becoming close.

On this last journey I got there early. I went first to Carraway's, since I had something I wanted to give Adda Korpi, but the cottage was empty. It was raining softly. Funeral weather, I thought glumly; the kind of setting Lillian Gish's director might have arranged for a burial scene. I made my way through beech trees and a sodden hedge to the mansion grounds, getting half-soaked in the process. The grass on the lawn was longer, and most of the château's windows were shuttered; rain had grayed the marble, it dripped off the ivy and plinked in puddles in tiny off-beat rhythms. The changes were small, but though Gatsby had been dead only ten days at that point, the place reeked of wet slate and abandonment. You got the feeling the hedges, the honeysuckle, even the frogs were holding their breath, waiting for the last humans to leave with evening so they could reclaim their own; pull down the cornices, invade the green lawns, turn this acreage back to the wild, fecund place of which, among all men, only the native Lenape had known the secrets.

I'd expected, because of the hundreds who had attended his parties, that hundreds would attend Gatsby's funeral, but I was wrong. The mourners huddling in the château's cavernous foyer consisted of a spindly Lutheran minister and a dozen people, most of whom were part of the Wolfshiem crew who had replaced Gatsby's staff after the Valente incident. I spotted a chubby fellow in thick glasses who looked vaguely familiar, but in the whole crowd I recognized only the neighbor, Carraway, and Mrs. Korpi. And Stella Wolfshiem.

Jordan was not there. Nor was Daisy Buchanan—though I reckoned she should have been. I still did not fully understand what happened the day Myrtle died, but if Jordan had been in the blue Ford with Tom Buchanan then, logically, the blond woman driving the cream-yellow phaeton must have been Daisy. Her hair was the same light shade of gold as Jordan's; and she was the only one with reason, after all, to drive by Wilson's garage, when the main road from the city to Long Island lay a quarter mile to the north. She knew about Myrtle, and must have wanted to catch a glimpse of her husband's mistress. But why did she switch cars with her husband? And what were they all doing in the city? And did she swerve into Myrtle on purpose?

Whatever the explanation, it no longer seemed important. Myrtle had run, of her own free will, into the phaeton's path; it would be impossible to prove for sure whether Daisy had swerved to hit or to avoid her. Jay's car had killed Myrtle, George had killed Jay, the affair was closed. Even if the cops found out Daisy was driving and pursued an investigation, Buchanan's lawyers would ensure any indictment got thrown out of court faster than you could say "arbitrary and capricious."

Judging by the look of their mansion, still dark and empty of life across the bay, the Buchanans had left town. Perhaps Daisy had gotten her wish and boarded a steamer for Europe. In contrast to all the elements that didn't add up in the affair, this one made sense.

Shielded from the day-to-day world by money, it seemed to me the rich always drifted as they pleased, like skiffs in a sheltered lagoon, immune from the oceanic gales that pummeled the rest of us. Daisy would feel guilt, no doubt, but whenever it popped up she would hop another gorgeous boat to another fabulous estate, and what happened to Myrtle and George, and to Gatsby, would again be lost to view behind the tapestry of her brocaded present.

None of this surprised me. What did surprise me was that, for the first time in years, I could not slap away the memory of what happened with a backhand of hard-earned cynicism; I could not torque myself into forgetting. A smolder had winked to life, deep inside my gut, and would not entirely go out. It had been so long since this kind of heat had touched me that for a while I did not even recognize the anger for what it was.

The emptiness of Gatsby's house rang around me as I waited, summoning more echoes of those I'd seen here. Meyer Wolfshiem had not come. Neither had Lillian Gish, or her director, or the famous novelist from Glen Cove and his ebullient Southern wife. Nor had the girls in yellow dresses, the predatory Brits, the woman who'd lost her tiara. Even the memory of their chatter, the music of their champagne glasses, the bubbles in their music seemed to have vanished utterly in that same held-breath of summer becoming fall.

I found myself thinking that a certain balance could be found in such poor attendance. What had made Gatsby remarkable was the power of his love for Daisy, or (as Jordan claimed) for the stability she represented. Those who'd thought him remarkable merely because of his opulence had vanished when that opulence dissolved.

Like them, I had been dazzled by the splendor of Gatsby; unlike them, I had also been awed by the drama of his affair. It was only when his life came crashing down that I could see another love had been as great as Gatsby's, or greater: that of George Wilson for his wife. One train—I remembered those words as the funeral party finally stirred—can hide another ...

I was driven to the cemetery with the other servants in Gatsby's station wagon. I made sure to sit in front so I would not sit where Young Sam had lain as he died.

After the usual rites, remarkable only for how tired they were, how representative of the doomed desire to find meaning in absence, I walked over to Adda Korpi and held out the envelope I had prepared. She stood there under a small flowered umbrella, her black servant's skirt soaked from the waist down, and stared at the envelope. Her cheeks were stiff with thoughts she had no wish to betray. She started to protest.

"It's not money," I told her in Finnish. "Please."

Reluctantly, she grasped the envelope. I put my hands in my pockets so she could not hand it back. "It's a present," I said, and it was, though I had included $100 cash for expenses. The envelope contained an open, one-way ticket on the Sweden-North America Line, New York to Stockholm, with a railway add-on to Helsinki, all for a grand total of $87. I had bought a cheaper ticket, second-class interior cabin on whatever ship she chose, in hopes that Mrs. Korpi would not be too shocked by the price, and seek me out to return it.

"Open it later," I told her. "It was good of you to come."

She held the envelope with both hands, so hard it crinkled; I had a feeling she knew what it contained. Her eyes were like old china, washed out and cracked. "He was nice to me," she said, "*Herra* Gatsby."

I nodded, trying not to think of her carrying that basket of heavy plates. I turned to find Stella standing behind me under an umbrella three times the size of Mrs. Korpi's.

"How come he isn't here?"

I meant Wolfshiem. She knew exactly what I meant.

"He doesn't like trouble. He didn't even want me to come. He only let me because of this." In an odd parallel to what I'd just done she held out an envelope; unlike Mrs. Korpi, I took it without a quibble.

"Guess I'm out of a job," I remarked, stashing the envelope in my trousers. She nodded. The usual southwest breeze blew black curls around her dark eyes and she blinked them away. She stood hipshot, and thrust out the umbrella in invitation. I stepped in close enough that I could feel the warmth of her body. One-handed, she dug a pack of cigarettes from her tiny purse, put one between her lips, and offered me another. I lit them both and we stood there smoking, listening to rain patter on the umbrella, hiss on the grass. The chubby and bespectacled fellow, I now realized, was the man who'd lain prostrate in Gatsby's library, exclaiming "Real books! Real books!" He was talking to Carraway, who wore his usual air of waiting for something else to happen. Whatever that might be, he clearly did not expect it from the chubby fellow.

Beside them a wiry old man in an ulster coat talked animatedly to the minister, showing him what looked like a daguerreotype, which he sheltered carefully under a plaid and broken-ribbed bumbershoot.

"Who's that?" I asked, pointing at the old man.

"Mister Gatz," she said. "Jay's father. He came from Minnesota, he shows everyone that daguerreotype."

"A portrait of Jay?"

"A picture of Jay's house." She looked up at me. "What will you do now?"

"I don't know," I said. She was looking at me in that way women have, aiming hard at one eye then the other. The glints of hazel, the shards of green in her irises that I'd first noticed at Gatsby's party shone clearer in the silvered light of rain. Her hands were held over her breasts, almost together, one holding the umbrella, the other her cigarette; the posture rounded her shoulders toward me in a shape so perfect for holding within the arc of another's arms that I almost tried: without my being aware, my body leaned forward perhaps five degrees and my lips advanced toward hers. But she did not move either toward me or away, and I stopped. We looked at each other for a few seconds more and in that look acknowledged both what drew us to each other and what had always kept us apart.

"I still want to take you out to lunch," I whispered. She shook her head and smiled. I had never noticed how her smile, though it only pulled up one corner of her lips, also opened a line at each side of her mouth; like two strings drawing a curtain, they made her appear more open, more vulnerable too. With the hand that held her cigarette she tapped my forearm softly, twice. It felt like farewell, it felt like regret, it felt like she'd wanted to touch me and would never touch me again.

Dropping her spent cigarette into the sodden grass she ground out the stub, unnecessarily, with the pointed toe of her shoe, and walked away.

—

Marcus took over the garage, or rather he took over the job of supervising the rum depot and its roster of guards under the cover of a filling station. Mike kept the coffeeshop going; thanks to the notoriety of the Wilson/Gatsby murders it was still attracting enough customers to make a profit. They said I could stay in my room over the depot but I declined. Everything there now reminded me of loss: of Gatsby, of Young Sam, of George and Myrtle—of Jordan a little, of Stella very much.

I missed *Daisy* too; she was sold or taken over in some gray deal by a different gang of rum-runners. The thought of her graceful lines, and the engines so lovingly maintained by Wilson, being used by the kind of people Wolfshiem did business with made me feel, with more heart than reason, that I had lost another friend.

I sold my phonograph to Mike for a quarter of its value and found a job in the only other community I had access to. Many of the New York tugs were run by Norwegians. They did not much care much for Finns, but they cared even less for everyone else. I rented a room in a Norwegian boarding house near the Red Hook docks and got a job as deckhand on the steam tug *Ryan XI* pulling barges between New Jersey and Brooklyn.

The work was hard, which I was used to on tugboats. It was also poorly paid. My company, Ryan Towing, had not raised crew wages since before the war and they fired anyone who complained: this I was not used to. A number of waterfront unions existed in New York harbor but they were small, disorganized and powerless. I approached Rolf Madsen, who was mate on another Ryan tug and also shop steward for non-licensed men in the New York Harbor Boatmen's Union, and mentioned we could put more pressure on owners if the various towboat unions organized under IWW, as the Duluth-Superior Watermen's Guild had done. Madsen turned (paradoxically) red, called me a Bolshevik, and came close to throwing me off his tug.

I kept quiet after that, partly to save my job, partly from a recurrence of surprise: because once again, although in a far more specific way than happened when I'd thought about how Wilson died, I found myself getting angry about such unfairness. And for the first time in a long while, I wished I could do something about it.

I hung onto my job through October. I got used to the hard work and low wages. I drank less, smoked less, my cough disappeared. The Norwegians disapproved of poker, so in the slack time between tows I reread Marcus Aurelius. "Loss is nothing else than change," I read. "The universal nature delights in change, and in obedience to her all things are now done well." I wasn't too sure about that last part but the cadence of the Stoic's lines pleased me overall and I picked out, as always, scraps of comfort from his meditations.

Yet for the first time since I got to New York, I found myself growing homesick. The few trees alive in Red Hook were losing their torched greens as the weather cooled. Though the cooling was minimal compared to how it happened in Minnesota, I suppose that winter reflex: of bringing home, of gathering; was at work in me. More and more often I thought of my parents, and what they might be doing for the upcoming holidays. I remembered the traditional Finnish start to Christmas, the feast of Saint Lucia on December 13th, when Miina Winikainen next-door, for whom Eiki and I had both lusted in vain, used to put on a white gown and a crown of candles to serve cardamom buns and mulled wine to her neighbors.

I thought of Christmas Eve with the candle-lit tree, the old, slow carols; and the snow, our deep Minnesota snow that killed so easily, but also transformed and softened. I thought that maybe, if the heart could juggle vacuums the way a tug's steam engine did, the losses I had suffered in this city might finally have balanced out the losses suffered in Minnesota. The level that resulted was one of grief, but it meant that one place was no more haunted than the other, and maybe I could go home again.

I had saved almost $6000 from rum-running. It was not money as Gatsby understood it but it was enough to help my parents, whether they wanted help or not. It was enough to support me comfortably for a year or two if, for example, I found cheap lodgings and volunteered as an organizer for the IWW. I knew from the papers that the Wobblies were still pretty active in Chicago. And I'd not forgotten that Wolfshiem had an office in Chicago, to which Stella sometimes brought documents.

Most importantly, I had enough money that I did not have to have to put up with the pressure the Ryan managers exerted to work long hours for low pay, and no bonus for overtime.

"You don't live forever": the words rang in my head as they had the night Myrtle Wilson died. So it was that one day, after working eighteen hours straight in a cold, stinging rain and 20-knot winds as we wrangled coal barges from Hoboken to the Peck Slip docks, I walked off the *Ryan XI*. Still in boots and greatcoat, I went to Pennsylvania Station and bought a ticket for Duluth....

Once the train had steamed past Yonkers, the forests turned the color of sunset, of milk splashed on gold—the color, I couldn't help remembering, of Jordan's hair, of Daisy Buchanan's too.

A little later, the forests' leaves grew scarce. We followed the tracks north through Albany. Past Rochester the sky took on a sheen of steel. Soon after Buffalo, as the train ran westward, parallel to the hard rule of Lake Erie, it began to snow.

Looking at the lake, I thought again of the boy who had rowed to the side of the *Tuolomee* as we lay anchored on the lee shore of a lake further west, who spoke of the great peril of staying where we were; of the hope we might share, as open and limitless as America, if only we would travel on.

Acknowledgements

THIS IS A NOVEL I've been longing to write for many years but it couldn't have seen the light of day, at least in its finished form, without help from family, friends and colleagues, in particular Jerome Murphy, Kathy Nora, Johan Van Der Meter, and especially Alexandre and Emilie Foy. Thanks are also due to New York City-based author and bartender Toby Cecchini for expert advice on what flappers and working people were drinking in 1922. Like everything else in the novel, the cocktails included are accurate for that era, but Toby has tweaked two recipes (French 75 and The Bee's Knees) to make them more palatable to modern tastes. Finally, I wish to thank UAW Local 7902 and International Workers of the World's Printing and Publishing Union 450 for their efforts in support of U.S. writers and teachers of writing; and, more generally, all organizers and activists of the progressive labor movement, past and present. To these idealistic people who, often at great personal cost, have tirelessly fought for the interests of the American worker, this book is respectfully dedicated.

About the Author

GEORGE MICHELSEN FOY's thirteen novels (the latest, *Enquête sur Kamanzi*, Editions Globophile, Paris, 2018; and *Mettle*, 2010, University Press of New England) were published by, among others, Bantam-Doubleday-Dell, Viking Penguin, University Press of New England, Bastei Lubbe (Germany): short fiction and essays with *Ep;phany Journal, Washington Square Review, Monkey Bicycle, Apeiron, Notre Dame Review, American Literary Review* et al. Of his novel *To Sleep with Ghosts* (Bantam / Doubleday), Nobel prize-winner Doris Lessing wrote, "[Foy is] a storyteller who, like Conrad, can compress into a tale you can't put down all the complexities of a time and place." Foy's long-form non-fiction has been published in *Harper's, Rolling Stone, Men's Journal, Slate* et al. His latest non-fiction book, *Run the Storm*, was published in May, 2018, by Scribner / Simon & Schuster. Another non-fiction work, *Finding North: How navigation makes us human*, came out with Flatiron / Macmillan in 2016. A non-fiction book on silence (*Zero Decibels: The Search for Absolute Silence*, Scribner) was published in 2011. A quartet of futurist novels, originally published by Bantam Spectra, is currently being reissued in e-book form by Lume Books UK. GM Foy was awarded a National Endowment for the Arts fellowship in fiction, and has won a Joe Gouveia Poetry award as well as awards in *Ep;phany Journal's, Foreword's, Fiction Factory's* and *Cutthroat Journal's* short-story contests. GM Foy lives in southeastern New England and Brooklyn and teaches writing at

NYU. At various times in a checkered career he was smuggled into Afghanistan with a rebel patrol and witnessed bombing raids on guerrilla camps in Central Africa; he also worked as factory-hand, magazine editor, agricultural laborer, commercial fisherman, watchkeeping officer on British tramp freighters, and as chief cream-pastry transporter for a cakes factory in West London.

Printed by Imprimerie Gauvin
Gatineau, Québec